Jane Austen's

MANSFiELD PARK

RETOLD BY AYISHA MALIK
ILLUSTRATED BY ÉGLANTINE CEULEMANS

HODDER

HODDER CHILDREN'S BOOKS

First published in Great Britain in 2020 by Hodder & Stoughton

1 3 5 7 9 10 8 6 4 2

Text copyright © Ayisha Malik, 2020
Illustrations copyright © Églantine Ceulemans, 2020

The moral right of the author has been asserted.

A CIP catalogue record for this book
is available from the British Library.

ISBN 978 1 444 95071 7

Typeset in Bembo by Hewer Text UK Ltd, Edinburgh
Printed and bound in Great Britain by Clays Ltd, Elcograf S.p.A

The paper and board used in this book
are made from wood from responsible sources.

Hodder Children's Books
An imprint of
Hachette Children's Group
Part of Hodder & Stoughton
Carmelite House
50 Victoria Embankment
London, EC4Y 0DZ

An Hachette UK Company
www.hachette.co.uk

www.hachettechildrens.co.uk

Mansfield Park, by Jane Austen, was first published in 1814.

This was the Regency era – a time when English society was sharply divided by wealth and women were expected to marry young.

The heroine of this story, Fanny, might have some things in common with modern readers, but she lived in a very different world.

You can find out more about Jane Austen and what England was like in 1814 at the back of this book!

MAIN CHARACTERS

MR PRICE
Father of nine. Mr Price lacks an education and prefers drinking to working.

MRS PRICE
Mother of nine. Mrs Price is disowned by her parents and siblings for eleven years for marrying beneath her social status.

MR WILLIAM PRICE
Fanny's younger brother and her closest sibling. He is a bright and capable young man, commissioned in the navy.

MISS FANNY PRICE
Our heroine! Sensible and modest, Fanny is the eldest of nine. She is adopted by the Bertram family and lives at Mansfield Park with them.

MISS SUSAN PRICE
Fanny's younger sister. Susan looks after all her siblings when Fanny moves to Mansfield Park.

LADY BERTRAM
Fanny's wealthy aunt who lives at Mansfield Park. She is a lazy woman who cares for her pet pug above all else.

SIR THOMAS BERTRAM
Lady Bertram's husband. Sir Thomas is the strict and stern patriarch of Mansfield Park.

MR TOM BERTRAM
The Bertram's older son. Tom is a gambling man and enjoys too much partying.

MR EDMUND BERTRAM
The Bertram's younger son. Edmund is training to become a clergyman. He is a well-mannered, handsome man and a close friend of Fanny's.

MISS MARIA BERTRAM AND MISS JULIA BERTRAM
Lady and Sir Thomas Bertram's daughters. Both Maria and Julia are vain and only think of themselves.

MRS NORRIS
Fanny's aunt. Mrs Norris has no children of her own and acts as a busybody around Mansfield Park.

MR JAMES RUSHWORTH
A wealthy but boring bachelor with eyes for Maria Bertram.

MR JOHN YATES
A friend of Tom Bertram who comes to visit Mansfield Park and proposes they put on a play.

DR GRANT
A vicar at Mansfield Parsonage, Dr Grant loves food more than anything else.

MRS GRANT
Married to Dr Grant. She is a cheerful woman who likes to matchmake.

MISS MARY CRAWFORD
Mrs Grant's younger sister, Mary comes to stay at Mansfield Parsonage and thinks Edmund is very dashing.

MR HENRY CRAWFORD
Mrs Grant's brother. Henry likes to use his charm to make women fall in love with him.

CHAPTER ONE

Fanny Price was unlucky enough to have been born into a poor family. Her strong-headed mother had fallen in love with a man who had no education and preferred drinking to work, and so, she'd been disowned by the family. Eleven years had passed without any communication between them. Fanny knew that she had cousins, aunts and uncles, but they all felt very distant – living a much grander life than the one she knew at home. But when Mrs Price fell pregnant with her ninth child, she decided – *finally* – that her family owed her some support. She wrote a letter to her wealthy sister, Lady Bertram, that was full of so much misery and *so many* children, and asked if the Bertrams might help her.

Lady Bertram and her husband, Sir Thomas, replied to Mrs Price with friendly advice, a small sum of money and some baby linen.

Mrs Price's other sister was married to a man called Reverend Norris. They lived near the Bertrams, though not in quite such a grand house. Mrs Norris was the most passionate of the sisters, and she sent very long letters filled with sympathy. But she couldn't help but feel this wasn't enough, and soon she was scheming of new ways to lighten the load for Mrs Price.

'Why don't we take over the care of one of her children?' she suggested one day. 'We could take the eldest daughter. Think of all the advantages she'd have, being brought up in this family? A good marriage, at least. What more could a lady want?'

Lady Bertram agreed without thinking too much about it. She liked it when other people had her thoughts for her.

Sir Thomas hesitated. *He* was thinking of his eldest sons, Tom and Edmund, and cousins falling in love. 'It happens all the time, after all, and our statuses ar—'

'Better for her to grow up *with* the children, so they see each other as brothers and sisters,' interrupted Mrs Norris. 'She won't be as good-looking as your beautiful Maria and Julia, but even if she *is*, think what would happen if Tom or Edmund met her ten years from now? She'd be quite *mysterious*.'

'You have a point,' Sir Thomas replied, thoughtfully.

'You are so considerate,' exclaimed Mrs Norris. 'I'll *never* love the girl as much as *your* children, but she is my sister's child and so I *must* help. You know I have a warm heart. I will write to my sister tomorrow and have it organised. My own trouble never matters to me.'

Sir Thomas agreed to the plan – happy that they were doing something good. 'She could become a very good companion for you, sister.'

'*Me?*' replied Mrs Norris. 'She can't live with me. Mr Norris couldn't bear the noise of a child.

His health, you know?'

Sir Thomas didn't know. He'd assumed that since Mrs Norris had no children of her own, and had suggested the plan, that Fanny would live with her. But Mrs Norris had other views. Lady Bertram, who was falling asleep on the sofa with her pug, had no opinion on the matter either way.

'I see,' Sir Thomas replied. 'Well, I suppose she'll have children her own age here at Mansfield Park.'

'Exactly, 'said Mrs Norris. 'I do hope for all our sakes that she's a good girl and realises how lucky she is.'

'There's no reason to think the worst,' Sir Thomas replied. 'But we must be prepared for her to be ignorant and ill-mannered. Still, these faults can be cured. If Maria and Julia were younger, I'd have reconsidered our plan, but they will be good role models for her. We will make her a part of the family but will have to remind her that she is *not* a Miss Bertram.'

Mrs Norris wrote the letter and Mrs Price was delighted, though a little surprised that they didn't want any of her lovely boys, instead. It was all settled, and everyone was now free to enjoy the idea of how kind they were, especially Mrs Norris, who would do her duty as an aunt without having to spend a penny.

CHAPTER TWO

Fanny, aged ten, had to hold back her tears when she met her aunt. They sat in the carriage and the old lady looked at Fanny up and down with her beady eyes.

'Well, there's nothing offensive about you, at least,' she said. 'I hope you know how lucky you are, being taken in like this?'

Fanny felt bad, but being taken away from her family and home seemed very *unlucky*. Her aunt talked at her the entire journey: *amazing* family, *beautiful* girls, such *handsome* boys! They approached Mansfield Park and the house's magnificent size filled Fanny with fear. How could she *ever* belong here?

She walked in behind her aunt, head low, taking deep breaths.

'Welcome, my child,' exclaimed Sir Thomas loudly, frightening Fanny further. 'How was your journey? Is your family well? Would you like something to eat? There, there, you're with a new family now . . .'

Fanny didn't know how to respond to Sir Thomas's thousand words per minute. Lady Bertram merely smiled, which Fanny preferred.

'Hallo, there,' bellowed Tom, the eldest Bertram boy, jumping out at Fanny with a flashing smile.

'Don't mind him,' added Edmund, giving Tom a look. 'Welcome to our home,' he added, offering his hand.

Slowly, she gave him hers. Maria, aged thirteen, and Julia, aged twelve, gave Fanny's outfit a quick once over. She was unimpressive enough for them both to start showing off how impressive they were.

Fanny stared at them all. Everyone was so good-looking and seemed well-mannered. She felt ashamed of her shabby clothes, her awkwardness and missed home even more. She *tried* to hold back the tears, but it was no good. They burst out, surprising the whole family. No one knew what to do.

'Maybe she needs rest?' suggested Sir Thomas.

So, Fanny was given a quick dinner and sent off to bed.

'Well, this isn't very promising,' said Mrs Norris. 'Even after everything I told her about being grateful. She'll get over it soon, I daresay.'

Unfortunately, it wasn't quite as soon as they'd all hoped. No one meant to be unkind, but no one went out of their way to make Fanny feel at home, either. The sisters were shocked that Fanny couldn't speak French or play an instrument or three, Lady Bertram's continued silence made Fanny feel like she had done something wrong, Sir Thomas's stern looks scared her, and her boy cousins were intimidating. Mrs Norris only added to all this by repeating how lucky Fanny should feel.

A whole week went by with Fanny secretly sobbing herself to sleep, until one day she was sitting behind the staircase having a good cry, when somebody interrupted her.

'*Fanny.*'

She jumped. It was Edmund, looking surprised and worried.

'What's *wrong*?' he asked.

He sat next to her and spoke so gently it made Fanny want to cry again.

'Nothing. I'm sorry. I'm fine.'

'Has someone said something?'

Fanny shook her head

'Are you ill?'

'No,' she replied.

He asked a hundred other questions to which she could do nothing but reply, 'no'. How could she explain how she was feeling?

'You don't have to be shy with me. I won't bite. I promise,' said Edmund.

This made Fanny smile.

'You miss home, don't you?' he asked.

Fresh tears fell down Fanny's cheeks as Edmund handed her his handkerchief.

'Come on, let's take a walk outside and you can tell me all about your family.'

The fresh air did Fanny good, and though it took a while (and many questions from Edmund) she began to tell him about her brothers and sisters, but especially her older brother, William.

'He said he'd miss me lots.'

'Of course,' replied Edmund. 'Who wouldn't miss such a lovely child like you? Why don't you write to him?'

'I promised I would, but . . .'

'But?'

She mumbled something.

'Sorry?' asked Edmund

'*But*,' she repeated, 'I don't have any paper or pens.'

Edmund tried not to laugh at just how shy she was.

'I'll give you everything you need. Come on,' he added.

He took Fanny to a room where she could write her letter. Edmund sat with her the whole time, even writing a note to his cousin and slipping some money in the seal for him. Fanny didn't have the words to show her thanks, while Edmund felt ashamed that the family hadn't done more to help her settle in.

After that day, Sir Thomas didn't scare Fanny as much, nor did Mrs Norris's voice fill her with dread. Tom, who at seventeen was as spirited as a young man with everything should be, sometimes gave Fanny presents and sometimes laughed at her. Plus, she came in handy as a third person in the girls' playtimes, even though they did think Fanny was stupid. She couldn't even put the map of Europe together! They didn't think about the fact that she'd never had a governess to teach her about such things. When they told their aunt, Mrs Norris, she simply replied, 'Well, girls. Not everyone can be as clever as you.'

This was the most moral guidance the girls were ever given, so who could blame them for being selfish? Their father, Sir Bertram, wasn't very affectionate, so they never showed their true colours to him, and Lady Bertram didn't have time for things like parenting. She was too busy sitting on the sofa, beautifully dressed, giving her attention to her beloved pug. So, the girls had everything except warmth and humility, which some might say is more important than knowing how to put a map of Europe together.

Years passed like this as Fanny grew up in her adopted family, not feeling a part of it, but not horrified by it any more either. As for *her* family, no one really thought of her, apart from William.

He came to spend a week with her before he was sent off to be a sailor. It was just as wonderful to be reunited with her brother as Fanny had imagined. She was dreadfully sad when the week came to an end, but thankfully Edmund was there to comfort her when William had to leave. With her brother's visit, and Edmund by her side, how could she not feel grateful for all of it?

Edmund's affection and attention didn't fade

over the years — even when he went off to school and then university to study. With all of this, how could she not love Edmund? He was the finest gentleman she had ever met and *would* ever meet.

CHAPTER THREE

The most significant thing *almost* happened to Fanny when she was fifteen. Her uncle, Reverend Norris, died and Sir Thomas felt that one positive thing could come out of his friend's death: now that Mrs Norris was alone, she could take Fanny.

Fanny had only just got over her luck at living at Mansfield Park. Now she was in danger of more luck than she could handle. Thankfully, it turned out that Mrs Norris had other ideas.

'I'm just a poor widow,' she exclaimed. 'You couldn't expect me to look after a child alone? And Fanny may *seem* sweet, but she could take advantage of a poor, kind woman like me.'

Sir Thomas was once again surprised by his sister-in-law. Especially because the only trouble Fanny ever gave was when she was asked to speak in front of more than one person.

Still, now that Mrs Norris was widowed, she had to leave the parsonage that was next to their home, but managed to get a place that was within walking distance. Edmund was expected to become a clergyman when he was full-grown, at which point the parsonage would be his, and, as with all clergymen, it would come with its own living wage. But in the meantime a Dr and Mrs Grant would live there. They were a very respectable couple – she was always in a good mood and he spent more time thinking about his dinner than he did about his sermons.

Sir Thomas had other worries, though. He had discovered that his eldest son, Tom, had been spending such vast sums of money on gambling and drinking that it was going to affect Edmund's inheritance. He sat Tom down one day and tried to explain things.

'Because of your debts, poor Edmund will have half the income that should have been his,' said Sir Thomas gravely.

Tom listened with some shame, which lasted about three and a half minutes. He felt sure that his father must be exaggerating, and he wasn't keen to change. But what he hadn't realised was that Sir Thomas had a plan to take Tom far away from temptation. He needed to deal with some business matters on the other side of the world, in Antigua, and, hoping that a change of scenery might change Tom's ways, Sir Thomas decided to take him too.

Their absence had very little effect on the household, except that since Maria and Julia were now free of Sir Thomas's restrictions they could regularly attend parties and balls. Fanny felt ashamed that she wasn't sadder with her uncle gone, but as

Edmund was able to deal with everything at home, things didn't quite fall apart.

A year passed and Sir Thomas was kept in Antigua, taking care of his business, but he sent Tom home, as any sensible parent might.

'Sir Thomas making it home alive looks less and less likely,' declared Mrs Norris, always the hopeful one.

Her fears, which she shared often, were soon forgotten when Maria and Julia came down, ready to go to another ball.

'Well, don't you both look beautiful,' said Mrs Norris admiringly.

'Very beautiful,' added Lady Bertram, who smiled vaguely at her daughters before getting back to her pug (she was going to stay at home, as usual). Maria was told she was beautiful so often, by everyone she knew, that she now fully believed she was perfect. Fanny couldn't help but admire her cousins' beauty, and their ease in social gatherings. It never occurred to her she was never asked to go with them, but she was happy to stay behind to keep Lady Bertram company, while Mrs Norris acted as chaperone to the Bertram sisters.

'We'll bring back all the gossip, as always,' Edmund told Fanny with a smile, as they all left.

At the ball, Mrs Norris immediately scanned the room, looking for a certain gentleman she had decided would make a suitable husband for Maria. It had recently occurred to Mrs Norris that Maria, with all her beauty and accomplishments, should get married − and who better than a responsible aunt to arrange things, since, with Sir Thomas away, her poor niece was practically fatherless.

'There! There is Mr Rushworth,' said Mrs Norris to Maria, pointedly, when she spotted him across the room.

Maria had met Mr Rushworth at a previous ball and felt that he had enough money and property to make him very handsome. Mr Rushworth believed the time had come for him to get married, and so thought he must be in love with Maria.

'Miss Bertram,' he said, as he approached them all. He shook everyone's hand, talked non-stop about how his carriage had needed fixing and so he and his mother had almost not come, before sensing that Maria was getting bored.

'I say! Let's dance, eh?' he said.

So, they did. Mr Rushworth had enough common sense to see that his partner was the most beautiful woman he'd ever met, and this was all the common sense necessary to make him a suitable husband, in Mrs Norris's eyes.

Soon, both families decided that the marriage would be a good thing. A letter was written to Sir Thomas for his approval, which was given, and all they had to do now was wait for him to return before the couple got married (if he didn't die first, of course).

Edmund was the only one who had reservations.

'Fanny,' he confided in his cousin one day. 'I'm afraid that Mr Rushworth's money is the only thing that keeps people from seeing how stupid he is.'

Fanny tried to name one good quality of Mr Rushworth's. 'He said nice things about my needlework the other day.'

Edmund raised his eyebrows. 'You really are

the kindest creature on earth.'

She lowered her face so he wouldn't see her blush.

'Maria should be able to decide her own happiness,' Edmund continued. 'I only wish it weren't based on the size of someone's wealth.'

Fanny agreed. But then, there never was a time when she didn't agree with Edmund. Everything he said and did was pleasing to her. If only he could know it.

CHAPTER FOUR

Dr and Mrs Grant seemed to have settled into the parsonage very nicely, but the Bertrams hadn't seen much of their new neighbours (perhaps because Mrs Grant was kept so busy by her husband's demands about dinner). However, this was soon to change with the arrival of Mrs Grant's brother and sister: Miss Mary Crawford and Mr Henry Crawford. Mary and Henry were both young, wealthy and attractive and so were welcome additions to the village.

Mrs Grant, being the loving older sister that she was, said, 'I've decided. Mary, you will marry Mr Tom Bertram and Henry, you will marry the young Miss Bertram – Julia. She's pretty and talented.'

Mary Crawford was ready to get married as long as the marriage entailed money. She was content to be living close to a family high in status. She had seen Tom Bertram and decided that if she fell in love, a handsome man with a modern home and five miles of park was a worthy catch.

Henry bowed and thanked Mrs Grant.

'Good luck, dear sister,' Mary said, laughing. 'You'll have to get someone from abroad for Henry. He's met every woman in England and no one's good enough. This terrible flirt will break the Bertram sisters' hearts.'

Mrs Grant looked shocked. 'Henry. I don't believe it.'

'You're much kinder to me than Mary,' replied Henry.

'I'm sure that the only reason you've not settled down yet is because you haven't met the *right* person.'

Mary laughed again, giving her brother an indulgent smile. 'We'll soon find out, won't we?'

The Crawfords and Bertrams got along immediately. Miss Crawford was pretty, but not so tall and fair that she'd outshine either of the Miss Bertrams, so they were free to be charmed by her without jealousy. They didn't think Mr Crawford handsome at all at first, but he had very good teeth and was well-spoken. By the second visit he was still plain but *very* charming. By the third visit the Miss Bertrams had forgotten they'd ever thought him plain – he was the best man they'd ever met! Since Maria was already engaged, it was assumed that Henry and Julia would get married, which was perfect since Julia was ready to have someone fall in love with her. Although, Maria didn't see anything *very* wrong with liking the company of a charming man like Mr Crawford, whether or not she was already engaged to another.

'Sister,' said Henry to Mrs Grant one evening. 'Although Miss Maria Bertram is prettier and more elegant than Julia, I've decided to like Julia best because you told me to.'

'You will prefer her in the end,' replied Mrs Grant, trying to ignore the twinkle in his eye.

'But I prefer her in the beginning!' he exclaimed.

'So you should, since Maria is engaged.'

'Ignore him, sister,' said Mary. 'One day he'll be taken in by a woman and it'll serve him right.'

'But I don't want him *taken in*,' Mrs Grant exclaimed. It was always the way with sisters: they wanted honourable women even for their dishonourable brothers.

'Everyone who gets married is taken in,' said Mary. 'Except for you, of course,' she added quickly.

In all the meetings between the families, Fanny was thought about once or twice. Mary wondered if she really was as sensible as she seemed, or just gave the appearance of it. Henry was too busy thinking about Maria to pay attention. He was well aware of how he'd catch Maria's eye and let the look linger, and she seemed to accept his flirtations. Who wouldn't enjoy the attention of an elegant, beautiful woman?

So, as with most unremarkable girls, Fanny was soon forgotten.

CHAPTER FIVE

The Crawfords regularly went to Mansfield Park for dinner, but since Tom had departed for a long stay in London this evening, Mary was prepared to feel a great hole in her life. Edmund, while well-mannered and handsome too, didn't exactly have the same spirit as Tom. Maria's fiancé, Mr Rushworth, had also joined them and talked mostly about his property, Sotherton, and the changes he wanted to make to it, turning to Maria every two seconds for her approval.

'If I'd had a fifteenth of the space you do, I'd have transformed the parsonage when I lived there,' exclaimed Mrs Norris. 'For I am naturally gifted at creating comfortable spaces,' she added, not considering the past ten years of discomfort she had caused Fanny.

'Shall we take some wine?' suggested Edmund, growing tired of Mr Rushworth's talk about his property.

But Mr Rushworth was not to be discouraged.

'I think my friend – who will help me modernise the house – would agree to take down the avenue that leads to the top of the hill. What do you think, my dear Miss Bertram?'

Maria glanced at him as if she didn't know what he was talking about. 'I've never seen the avenue.'

Fanny, who was sitting next to Edmund, said, 'It seems a pity to change things when Sotherton sounds like such a wonderful place. Changing anything from its original form feels a shame. I'd love to see it as it is now, but I don't suppose I will.'

Mary was listening to Fanny and interjected. 'Gosh, I should hate that. No, only show me when a change is complete. My uncle once re-did his home and took me to see it while renovations were being done – it was *awful*, I was furious with him. But it was typical of him, really. His decisions have always been . . . well, let's just say . . . questionable.'

Edmund usually liked Mary's liveliness but was uncomfortable at how frankly she spoke about her uncle. It suited him that she soon changed the subject.

'My harp is to be delivered soon, at last,' she said. 'It was such a to-do getting it from London. I was amazed how difficult it was to get a horse and carriage for hire in the village. It's quite set in its ways.'

'We are, I'm afraid,' said Edmund. 'The harp is by far one of my favourite instruments. I hope I can hear you play it very soon.'

Fanny also expressed a wish to hear it.

'Of course! I'll play for you both,' said Mary. 'Please tell your brother that my harp is arriving. He knows I was miserable without it.'

'I will when I have a reason to write to him,' replied Edmund.

'Brothers are so odd,' said Mary. 'Mine tells me everything but he'll never write me more than two words.'

Fanny coloured. 'Not *all* brothers,' she said, quietly.

Edmund explained that William, Fanny's older brother, wrote to her often and in detail.

'You might have heard of him, Miss Crawford, since you know so many people in the navy,' Edmund added.

'Only ones of superior rank.'

'It is a noble profession,' said Edmund thoughtfully.

'Yes, but it's not the kind of lifestyle I'd like,' Mary added.

Edmund changed the subject to her harp again while conversations of Mr Rushworth's property went on.

'Henry,' said Mrs Grant. 'You're very good at this sort of thing. You must help Mr Rushworth.'

Maria Crawford's eyes lit up. 'Oh, yes. You should get Mr Crawford's advice,' she said, rather too quickly. 'Don't you think?' she added to her fiancé.

Mr Rushworth did think, just as Maria wanted him to.

'It'd be my honour,' said Henry, stealing a glance at Maria.

'We should all go and give our opinion on it,' added Mrs Norris. 'People say I'm a woman with great taste, though I try not to show off.'

So, it was agreed and everyone was delighted with the plan, except for Edward, who stayed quiet.

★ ★ ★

'Well, Fanny,' said Edmund the following morning. 'What do you think of Miss Crawford?'

'I like her a lot,' Fanny replied. 'She is so lively and pretty. But . . .'

'Yes?'

'I just thought she shouldn't have spoken about her uncle like that.'

Edmund nodded. 'I'm glad you picked up on that. Just as I did.'

'She sounded very ungrateful.'

'I'm sure she has the right to. It sounds as if he treated Henry much better than he did her. She must have felt it. But still . . . she shouldn't have spoken like that about him in public. She is both witty and elegant, though.' Edmund smiled at Fanny. 'I'm glad you agree with me.'

Mary's harp finally arrived, and Edmund went to visit, as promised. Her elegance and beauty were only heightened by her musical talent.

Edmund had not realised that, after a week of regular visits, he was practically in love. As for Mary, Edmund did not charm or flatter like his brother. He was stubborn and was so sensible he should be considered dull. Except he wasn't. Mary liked seeing him and she could not understand why.

CHAPTER SIX

Fanny was surprised that Edmund chose to spend so much time with Mary, and that he seemed to no longer notice her ungracious comments. Fanny would listen to him compliment her after every visit, but felt mean for trying to highlight the things Mary would say which were alarming, so she kept quiet.

Two weeks after Mr Rushworth had mentioned it, the plan to go to Sotherton was set. They would be taking Henry's carriage.

'I hope Fanny's going too?' said Edmund.

'Heavens, why?' said Mrs Norris. 'She's not expected. And she must stay with your mother.'

Lady Bertram nodded. Fanny was, unhappily, the type of person who was insignificant yet necessary at the same time.

'Mother,' said Edmund. 'You can have no objection to Fanny going if you don't need her.'

'No, dear, but I *do* need her.'

'Not if I stay with you instead,' he offered.

There was an outcry at this. How could they do without *him*? He wasn't to be deterred though, until Mrs Grant said *she* would stay with Lady Bertram.

Fanny's affections for Edmund, which were already quite extraordinary, were increased ten-fold.

The morning of the visit came and Mrs Grant saw them off in the carriage.

'Julia, you should sit with Henry, as there won't be room for you all otherwise.'

Maria's face crumpled. Every time she saw Henry turn to her sister and smile, or any time Julia would laugh, she'd feel a stab of jealousy. The entire journey Maria felt in *very* poor spirits, until they approached Sotherton. It was so pleasing to look at, everyone complimented it so much, that her heart fluttered with all the energy one could expect of pride and vanity.

The party was shown around Sotherton; Maria was so pleased with it she had almost forgiven Julia for sitting next to Henry. They had all gone to visit the family chapel, when Mary said to Edmund and Fanny, 'I think it's a bit of a bore to *expect* people to pray every day at a certain time. Much better to do it in private. There's so much to distract when in a congregation.'

Fanny went red and glanced at Edmund. It took him a few moments to reply. 'A person distracted in a congregation would be just as easily distracted alone.'

Mary smiled her playful smile and all Edmund's seriousness seemed to have vanished.

In the meantime, Mr Rushworth and Maria were standing by the altar, as Julia noted to Henry.

'Don't they look like they should get married here and now?' she said, believing that she and Henry weren't too far behind them. Henry, however, smiled and stepped towards Maria, saying in a low voice, 'I don't like you so close to the altar.'

Maria's heartbeat quickened but she tried to keep her composure. 'Even if you gave me away?'

Henry gave her a meaningful look and whispered, 'That would be very awkward for me . . .'

Julia had turned around to the others. 'If only Edmund were ordained already! He could marry Maria and Mr Rushworth now.'

She'd clearly forgotten about her poor father, still on the other side of the world.

Mary visibly coloured. 'You're to join the clergy?'

'Yes,' Edmund replied gently.

Mary would have kept her thoughts about congregational prayers to herself if she had known.

They all made their way to the shrubberies, splitting into groups. Poor Julia's fate had turned and she was now stuck with her aunt, while the young people went on ahead.

They had been walking a while and Fanny was tired, so Edmund and Mary rested with her on a bench.

'I think you are made for something better than being a clergyman,' Mary said to Edmund eventually.

'It is an important calling,' Edmund replied. 'And one that I feel privileged to undertake.'

'But not *important* enough,' said Mary.

'Leading people in morality, helping them with their spirituality, isn't important?' he replied, with good humoured passion.

'*You*, I believe, were meant for something grander. Perhaps the law? There's still time.'

'Oh no,' interjected Fanny. 'Edmund would hate that.'

'Well, you've convinced Fanny,' said Maria, getting up. 'I must walk. Resting tires me!'

Edmund paused before he stood up too. 'I wish I could convince you, too.'

Mary looked at him longer than was proper and with a playful smile said, 'I do not think you will, I'm afraid.'

Fanny also stood up, but Edmund insisted that

she continue to rest, and so she was left watching Edmund and Mary as they walked out of sight.

It was twenty minutes before Mr Rushworth, Maria and Henry found Fanny.

'You've been used very badly, being left behind like this,' declared Maria.

Mr Rushworth nodded eagerly. The trio rested with Fanny until Maria noticed a gate up ahead, which she decided she wanted to go through.

'We'd see the house perfectly from there,' agreed Henry.

But a distraught Mr Rushworth didn't have the key. Maria was so adamant, though, that he was obliged not to keep a lock on her happiness and went to fetch it.

Fanny shifted in her seat, uncomfortable being left behind with Maria and Henry, and their conversation.

'You and Julia seemed to be all laughter on your way here,' said Maria to Henry.

'Well, she's easily amused.'

'Unlike me?' Maria asked.

'You, Miss Bertram, are a much more difficult creature to satisfy.'

Maria, pleased with this, stood up and looked past the gate. 'Mr Rushworth is taking his time, isn't he?'

'Here, look,' replied Henry. 'There's a gap. I could help you get past and Mr Rushworth could meet us up ahead.'

Fanny, who felt that this was all wrong, said, 'But what if he can't find you?'

'Nonsense,' said Maria. 'You'll tell him exactly where we've gone.'

Before Fanny could say any more, Henry and Maria were already on the other side of the gate, leaving Fanny alone once again. She couldn't help but feel that they had both behaved very badly. She wondered whether Edmund had forgotten her, but her heart lifted when she heard more footsteps approach.

It was Julia. 'Where are Maria and Henry?' she asked, barely acknowledging that poor Fanny was alone.

Fanny explained and then asked, 'Have you seen Edmund or Mary?'

'That was a pretty trick,' Julia exclaimed, ignoring Fanny's question as she went to follow Henry and Maria.

'Wait for Mr Rushworth. He'll be back with the key any minute,' called out Fanny.

'I've had enough of that man for one morning,' said Julia, who scrambled past the gate and was out of sight within moments.

Fanny was now faced with the trial of Mr Rushworth appearing five minutes later and having to explain what had happened. Poor Mr Rushworth had been used even worse than she had.

'I see,' he said after a few moments, looking unhappy and annoyed.

'Maria asked me to stay so I could pass the message to you,' added Fanny, hoping that she might at least make him feel better.

'I don't think I will follow them,' he said and sat down next to Fanny gloomily.

They both sat in silence.

'Miss Price, what do you think of Mr Crawford? Everyone seems to adore him. I can't see why, he's hardly taller than five foot eight.'

'I don't think he's handsome,' Fanny replied.

'We were better off without the Crawfords, in my opinion,' he added.

Fanny couldn't deny this, so just kept quiet. He stood up and walked towards the gate. Fanny, seeing this as a sign of him giving in, said, 'It'd be a shame to have got the key, only to miss out on seeing the gardens with them.'

He nodded. 'You're quite right. And though Maria should have waited for me, what is done is done, yes?'

Fanny smiled encouragingly as she watched Mr Rushworth leave too. By now, she was so used to people leaving her, she didn't feel bad about it. Fanny's thoughts returned to Edmund and Mary and she became determined to find them.

She discovered them, having forgotten her, sitting and laughing comfortably under a tree. It filled Fanny with pain.

'Oh, Miss Price,' cried Mary. 'It's all my fault.'

'No, Fanny, honestly, we quite lost track of time – it's entirely mine,' added Edmund.

'I'm sorry, I kept your cousin all to myself. I'm awfully selfish, but since there's no cure for selfishness, you must forgive me,' said Mary.

Fanny had little choice.

When they all went into the grand Sotherton house for dinner, it seemed clear to Fanny, by looking at Mr Rushworth and Julia, that she was not the only dissatisfied person. Julia's dissatisfaction, however, didn't last long after Henry came up to her and said, 'I hope I will have my companion for the carriage on the way home?'

Maria watched them and looked unhappy, while Mr Rushworth seemed much more content about the seating arrangement.

'Well, Fanny,' said Mrs Norris on the ride home. 'What a wonderful day it's been for you! You should be grateful to me and your aunt for letting you come.'

Once Mrs Norris stopped talking, everyone was left to wonder whether the day had brought more pain or pleasure. And everyone, as can be imagined, came up with a different answer.

CHAPTER SEVEN

'Girls,' said Mrs Norris over breakfast. 'We've just received a note that your father will return in November. He might make it back alive, after all.'

This news cast a shadow over Maria and Julia, but it was a much harsher prospect for Maria, who would finally have to marry Mr Rushworth. There was no denying that she had fallen very much in love with Henry. To keep herself from getting depressed, she believed that *surely* something would happen to delay her father's return, so she could carry on the simpler matter of being engaged to one man while being in love another.

The Crawfords dined at Mansfield Park that

evening. Afterwards, Mary went to stand by Edmund and Fanny who were by the window. 'Your sister will finally be able to marry,' she said, looking over at Henry, Maria and Mr Rushworth at the pianoforte. 'And *you* shall take your orders, and enter the church.'

'Yes,' replied Edmund.

'Oh, to be a clergyman,' she replied. 'Nothing to do but eat, read the newspaper and quarrel with his wife.'

'Your opinion of them is shaped by what you've heard others say, rather than your own experience, I think,' said Edmund.

'Well, and living with one . . . But anyway, if an opinion is general, then it's usually correct.'

'Oh no,' said Fanny. 'William talks so highly of the clergymen in Antwerp.'

'I wouldn't wish *you* to be the wife of a clergyman,' said Mary.

'If she were,' replied Edmund, 'there'd never be a reason to quarrel with dear Fanny.'

Just then, Mary was called by Maria and went over to the piano.

'She is an enchanting lady, isn't she?' said Edmund to Fanny as he looked admiringly at Mary. 'If only she'd been brought up a little better.'

'Yes,' agreed Fanny. They were quiet for a moment until Fanny said softly, 'The stars are quite magnificent this evening,' and they both gazed out of the window at the brilliant night sky. 'When there is such beauty in the world, it's hard to believe there is any wickedness in it.'

Edmund smiled. 'I wish all people were as enthusiastic as you about nature.'

'You're the one who taught me to appreciate it.'

Edmund turned his back to the window, hearing Mary playing the piano. He was already walking away from Fanny, leaving her alone, when Mrs Norris noticed her and exclaimed, 'Move away from the window! What if you caught a cold? Then what would Lady Bertram do?'

Indeed, what would any of them do?

By August, Tom returned from London with all the liveliness that, for Mary, had made him preferable to Edmund. But not any more! She now felt Edmund was superior to Tom in every way, and it was very annoying. Even if Tom inherited Mansfield Park tomorrow, and asked for Mary's hand in marriage, she would not accept it.

Henry had been called away for two weeks to Norfolk, and what a dull two weeks it was for the Miss Bertrams. They didn't understand that their feelings – one of which included Julia's severe jealousy of Maria – were inappropriate. And Henry was too busy feeding his ego to change his behaviour towards the sisters, or to stay away. So, when there were no ladies in Norfolk to compare to the Miss Bertrams, he returned to Mansfield Park to continue his hobby of heartbreak.

His return was a relief to Maria, who had had quite enough of Mr Rushworth's talk of sport and boasting about his dogs, and Julia who, un-engaged, felt that she had more of a right to miss Henry. Each sister believed themselves to be preferred by

Henry: Julia because of Mrs Grant's suggestions, and Maria because Henry told her so himself.

Since that day at Sotherton, Fanny couldn't help but observe each sister whenever Henry was around. She seemed to be the only one who found anything to dislike.

'I'm surprised he's back so soon, given he's used to more lively places than Mansfield Park,' said Fanny one day to Edmund, trying to give a subtle voice to her worries. 'He's such a favourite with Maria and Julia.'

'Hmm,' said Edmund. 'I believe he prefers Julia. Any faults he might have could be smoothed over with a serious engagement.'

Fanny hesitated. 'Sometimes . . . I wonder whether he would prefer *Maria,* if she weren't engaged.'

Edmund smiled. 'I can see why you might think that, but often men give their attention to an intimate friend or relation of the lady they admire to gain a better understanding of them.'

Fanny tried to ignore her suspicions but could not help detecting the hint of a smile from Julia after Henry had said something here, the passing of look between Henry and Maria there.

It was the first time she had doubted Edmund's opinion on anything.

CHAPTER EIGHT

Soon after Tom's return, a so-called friend, John Yates, came to stay. John had all the superficial liveliness that appeals to some. He'd come to Mansfield Park because he had been taking part in a play, *Lover's Vows*, which had to be cancelled because someone was inconsiderate enough to have a family member die.

John filled everyone in on how hard done by he was that *Lover's Vows* had been abandoned.

'Come now,' said Tom to his friend. 'Let's put on a play here!'

There was nothing like the theatre to inspire young minds.

'Really?' exclaimed John. 'We wouldn't need much. Any room in this house would do.'

'And it could just be a short performance,' added Henry keenly. 'It'd be great fun, no?' he said, turning to Maria and Julia, without it being clear which sister he was addressing.

'We'd need a curtain,' said Tom. 'For a sense of occasion.'

'I think we should stick to Henry's idea of a simple performance,' added Maria.

Edmund, who until now had been listening with some alarm, said, 'A mere performance? Surely not. We must have a stage with a pit and boxes and don't forget a gallery or two . . .'

'Edmund,' said Julia, 'don't be so negative. You love a good play.'

'Yes, to see *real* acting and, I'm sorry to offend, *real* actors.'

Edmund wanted to add how inappropriate it was for gentlemen and women to engage in such a thing, but had to bite his tongue since he didn't want to offend Tom's friend.

No one seemed to pay attention anyway, and carried on with their planning with all the buzz and excitement that new ideas generally inspire. Tom wanted a comedy, Henry and the Bertram sisters preferred a tragedy, but either way, everyone

was convinced that they'd find *something* that would satisfy them all.

Later that night, Edmund was in the drawing room, standing by the fire while Fanny attended to Lady Bertram. Tom came bouncing in from the billiard room.

'Awful room that is,' he exclaimed. '*But* . . . perfect as a theatre!'

'You can't be serious about carrying on with this scheme?' said Edmund as Tom approached the fire.

'Of course I am.'

'It's not proper,' replied Edmund. 'Not with father away, and then you have to think about Mary Crawford and her situation as a single lady. It might be very bad for her reputation. Plus, you know it's not the right thing for a family like ours. People look up to us, and we shouldn't betray their trust by – literally – acting in a way that's not proper.'

'Nonsense! It's just *us*, little brother. And father would be happy to have us do something to keep our poor mother's mind occupied. She must be so anxious about him returning safely. Isn't that right, Mother?'

The brothers looked over at Lady Bertram, lying on the sofa, a picture of health, gently nodding off to sleep.

'Yes, Tom, she seems very anxious,' replied Edmund.

'Don't be such a bore. I won't have you spoiling the fun for the rest of us.'

'Father has a strict sense of what is right for ladies and gentlemen.'

'I know our father as well as you do, Edmund, and I'll take responsibility for it all, thank you.'

There was no reasoning with Tom.

'If you must,' said Edmund, displeased. 'All I'll say is — don't spoil our father's home by turning this into a theatre.'

Tom put his hand up. 'Say no more. Just a simple stage, all done with hardly any expense.' And with that, Tom walked out of the room, leaving Edmund poking at the fire angrily. Fanny had heard everything and felt exactly as Edmund did. There was a time and place for everything, and with the head of the house, Sir Thomas, away, taking on a decision like this without his approval seemed disrespectful.

'Maybe they won't find a play to suit them?' she offered.

'No, they'll find something. I'll have to try and talk my sisters out of it. Aunt Norris won't like the scheme either, but no one will listen to her.'

Edmund tried to speak to Maria and Julia, but they felt if their mother had no objection, then there was no reason he should! In the midst of Edmund's attempt to convince his sisters, Henry came in and announced how delighted Mary was with the plans. Maria looked at Edmund as if to say, *you can't disagree if Mary is on board.* And so he kept quiet.

Mrs Norris objected for about five minutes before her eldest nephew and nieces talked her out of her doubts. Soon she decided it would be a good thing to come and stay at Mansfield Park to assist the youngsters. She wondered why she'd ever had any doubts about it – the plan was perfect for everyone.

CHAPTER NINE

Fanny had been right. No one could agree on a play. Meanwhile, the carpenter Tom hired to build the set had altered his plans twice, costing far more than had been intended. The material for the curtain had arrived and the housemaids were stitching it and *still* the play was undecided. Tom and Mary were the only ones who wanted comedy. Then, of course, everyone *had* to be a main character, so all the usual plays were binned just as soon as they were suggested. Until Tom exclaimed, 'What about *Lover's Vows*? A part for everyone,' he added. 'The tragic heroes and the comics.'

No one could believe they hadn't thought of it before, especially John Yates, who could now complete the play he'd had to abandon. The job of assigning characters was underway. Fanny was doing some embroidery quietly in the drawing room while Maria, Julia, Tom, Henry and John tried to organise things. Maria was determined to be Agatha, and so had set about giving the role of the Baron to Mr Yates. This left the role of Frederick – Agatha's beloved – for the only person she had in mind. But Julia *also* meant to be Agatha.

'What about Miss Crawford?' exclaimed Julia.

'She'll be happy with anything,' replied Henry.

'She *must* be Amelia,' said Tom. 'And one of my sisters will be Agatha.'

There was a tense pause as Henry pretended to go over the first act of the play, before he said, 'It can't be Miss *Julia* Bertram.' He tried to seem objective. 'I'll be in a fit of giggles at you playing a serious role, considering how much we've laughed!'

But it didn't matter how well he tried to dress it up, Julia saw Maria's suppressed smile and finally *knew* he preferred her sister.

'Quite right,' said Tom. 'Maria will be Agatha. Julia can be the old country woman.'

'What?' exclaimed John. 'Your sister deserves better than that.'

'Agreed,' said Henry. 'She must be Amelia. The perfect model of grace, I think.'

Julia softened a little.

'No, no, no,' said Tom. 'Miss Mary Crawford will be Amelia, and that's that!'

'I don't care for Amelia, anyway,' exclaimed Julia. 'She's a horrible character and I'd rather die than play her.'

With that, she swept out of the room, leaving an awkward silence behind her.

'I'd give the part to my sister, but she'd play the part even *worse* than me,' Maria said quietly to Henry, who properly contradicted her.

Soon enough, Maria wished to go with Henry to personally offer the part of Amelia to Mary, who was at the parsonage, while Tom and John went to discuss the practical side of the production. Fanny was left alone and so she picked up the volume of *Lovers' Vow*. She was shocked. Surely they couldn't know the kind of play they were taking part in. The characters! The language! It was all so improper for modest ladies and well-mannered gentlemen.

Tom could not have known what he was suggesting, and Fanny only hoped he *would* realise before Edmund found out.

CHAPTER TEN

Mary accepted her role happily and Mr Rushworth was to play a character called the Count, just as Maria had hoped.

'I hate the idea of all those fine clothes!' he said, imagining how handsome he'd look in a purple velvet cape.

He was so taken by the forty-two lines he would get to speak that managing his feelings regarding Henry's role as Maria's beloved in the play wasn't half as difficult as Maria thought it would be. All was finally looking to go ahead when Edmund, who had been out all morning, returned home and entered the dining room.

'*Lovers' Vows* is the play!' announced Mr Rushworth.

Edmund stood still in surprise and could only look at his brother and sisters. Maria blushed, in spite of herself. Tom was soon called out to attend to the carpenter and was followed by Mr Yates and Mr Rushworth, so Edmund turned to his mother, aunt, Fanny, and sister.

'Now that Mr Yates isn't here, I must tell you how *improper* this is. Maria, when you know what the play is about, I am sure you'll agree with me.'

'I *do* know and I find nothing wrong with it. Not with a little bit of editing and cutting, here and there.'

Edmund was agitated. 'You must talk them out of it. Your opinion is always respected. You have to lead by example – tell them how unsuitable the whole thing is for families of good upbringing.'

Maria wavered a little, since she did like to lead. 'Edmund, you're being too serious!' she said, finally.

'Don't act in anything improper, dear,' said Lady Bertram. 'Sir Thomas would not like it. Fanny, do ring the bell for supper.'

'Father will *not* like it at all,' he answered, stopping Fanny from ringing the bell.

'If I were to bow out then Julia would simply take my place,' replied Maria. 'Anyway, if we try and find a *proper* play then there'd be nothing at all!'

'Precisely,' said Mrs Norris. 'All this preparation and my being useful would be a waste of time and money.'

No more could be said, as Tom returned and Edmund didn't want to undermine his older brother, even though he knew he was right about this.

Dinner was quiet, aside from Mr Rushworth talking about his character's fine clothes and forty-two lines, and John Yates trying to distract Julia from her misery.

But, after dinner, Henry and Mary came up

from the parsonage to join the family in the drawing room and energies for the play renewed as the cast went to a table in the corner to discuss it.

'But wait a minute,' said Mary. 'Who will play my character's love, Anhalt? Nobody has been given that part yet.'

Mr Rushworth told her he had chosen the character of the Count already, 'Even though I hate all those fine clothes.'

'Oh, quite understandable. A woman as forward as Amelie would frighten most men,' she replied.

Tom could not play him because he was the butler and had a scene with Anhalt.

'What about your brother?' whispered John.

'*I'm* not going to ask him,' said Tom.

Mary, after a while, moved to sit with Edmund and Fanny by the fire.

'They have no use for me at their table,' she said to Edmund. 'What would you have me do, without anyone to play Anhalt?'

'I'd change the play.'

'Yes, but it all seems set to me.' She paused, smiling archly. 'Since Anhalt is a clergyman, *you* would do very well to play the part.'

'To *play* a clergyman would be the most loathsome thing to an actual man of the cloth,' replied Edmund.

Maria was suitably embarrassed and went quiet, before moving to speak to Mrs Norris.

'Fanny!' called out Tom. 'We need you.'

Fanny got up, thinking she was needed for an errand, when Tom added. 'No, no, not now. We need you to be the cottager's wife. Good girl.'

Fanny went bright red. Her heart beat so fast she could barely hear herself when she exclaimed, 'Never!'

'Oh, don't be silly, Fanny. It's a small part.'

'Exactly,' added Mr Rushworth. 'Think of me with my forty-two lines to learn.'

'It's not that,' she said, shocked that all eyes were on her. 'I couldn't possibly act.'

'You don't need to,' replied Tom. 'I'm the cottager's husband so will tell you what to do, push you about and you'll be done.'

'But . . . but . . .' Fanny had grown increasingly agitated and looked at Edmund for help.

He could only smile at her encouragingly, not wishing to interfere further with his brother.

'We'll give you a few wrinkles, a brown gown and you'll be the perfect old lady.'

Fanny was overwhelmed. 'Please don't make me.'

But now everyone was pressing Fanny, until she was close to what felt like a panic attack, when Mrs Norris spoke in an angry, audible whisper. 'Don't make such a drama when everyone is asking just *one* thing of you.'

'Do *not* force her to do something she doesn't wish to, Aunt,' spoke Edmund, who also felt angry now.

'I'm not *forcing* her, just pointing out that she's being very ungrateful and stubborn.'

Edmund grew too angry to speak, but Mary looked at Mrs Norris in shock.

'I don't like this table, I'm very hot here,' Mary said suddenly and left her seat to go and sit by Fanny, whose eyes brimmed with tears.

'Don't worry, Miss Price. Everyone is being very cross this evening. Let's forget about it.'

Mary, with this action, had recovered any of the favour that she might have lost with Edmund. And though Fanny did not care for Mary, she appreciated her kindness. Mary carried on speaking with Fanny, asking about her brother and paying all kinds of attention to her which had never occurred before.

'It won't do,' said Tom. 'We'll have to get someone from outside to play Anhalt.'

Mary glanced at Edmund.

'Charles Maddox will do it,' added Tom.

Mary simply said, 'I don't mind who it is, but a total stranger would be the worst. I've met Charles Maddox once, I think. I suppose he'll have to do.'

She leaned into Fanny and added, 'I'll cut some of his lines, and mine, before we rehearse together. It'll be disagreeable and not what I expected, but there we are.'

CHAPTER ELEVEN

Poor Fanny awoke the following morning with a heavy head and heart. To be called *ungrateful and stubborn*. She dressed and went to the East Room. She'd been given it because it was too small for anyone else to use, and Mrs Norris didn't object, as long as Fanny didn't get a fire in it.

Here, Fanny had everything she could want: her books, some plants, a writing table and things that she'd collected over the years, usually given to her by Edmund or her brother William. *Had* she been unreasonable? She could not make up her mind, when there was a knock on the door.

It was Edmund. Her heart felt calmer. 'I need your advice, Fanny.'

'*Mine*?' she said, surprised.

'Yes. This whole play scheme gets worse and worse and now they have some Charles Maddox coming here. I don't know anything about him, but I can't allow it.' He paused. 'There's nothing for it. *I* must play Anhalt.'

Fanny was shocked.

'I know. I don't like it either,' said Edmund. 'Firstly, it's as if I'm completely changing my mind, but having a stranger coming into the privacy of our home . . . such intimacy. Think about poor Miss Crawford, having to act with someone she doesn't know.'

Fanny hesitated. 'Is this really the answer? It feels like such a triumph for the others!'

'Not when they see my terrible acting. Anyway, by giving them this I'll at least have some control over the play, they'll be so grateful.'

'I see.'

'Do I have your approval, Fanny? I need it. If I don't, I won't trust my own thoughts.'

Fanny felt overwhelmed again, but this time at the honour her cousin gave to her opinion. 'It still feels wrong.'

'I thought you would think more about Miss Crawford's feelings,' he said. 'I certainly do, after seeing how she was with you yesterday.'

Fanny tried to be warmer and nodded. 'She *was* very kind.'

'Then it's done. I'm sure this is a better option. I just needed to speak with you about it first. I shall be on my way now to tell Miss Crawford, and everyone else, and leave you to your reading.'

He left the room, but there was no reading to be done. How could Edmund be so inconsistent? Wasn't he lying to himself? Fanny felt it was all Mary's fault – without her plea, Edmund would certainly have stayed out of the whole business. Fanny was sorry for her own mistrust, but she was sure Mary knew

Edmund would have been able to hear her last night when she spoke about the embarrassment of acting with a stranger, and was counting on him feeling that he ought to save her. It all felt miserable.

Tom and Maria *were* triumphant, but only in private. In public, they were all measured smiles. Mary Crawford was so delighted that Edmund couldn't help but feel he *had* done the right thing.

'Now, maybe Fanny will oblige us too,' said Tom, as Mr Rushworth sat and started counting Edmund's lines for him.

'No, she is determined,' replied Edmund.

'Fine!'

Not another word was said, but Fanny felt in constant danger of being hounded. She needn't have worried. Mary insisted that Mrs Grant play the part of the cottager's wife, and, after a few objections made by Mrs Grant, as was proper, she agreed. Everyone rejoiced further, aside from

Fanny. She couldn't accept Edmund's unsteadiness, his looks of happiness, or bear Mary's friendliness. And even though she would rather die than take part in the play, she couldn't help but feel that she was the only one without *any* importance.

The only person who suffered as much as Fanny was Julia. She couldn't get over Maria's self-satisfaction or the way Henry had used her. The sisters used to get along when there was nothing to test them. But Maria didn't think of Julia's pain, nor Julia of the situation her sister was getting herself into. True affection had always been lacking, so neither felt any real concern for the other. Instead, Julia wanted to make everyone as miserable as she was. Mr Yates tried to comfort her and Henry tried to be as thoughtful as a man who didn't care about a woman could, but after two or three days he gave up.

Of course, nothing is consistent. Soon everyone became irritable. Another carpenter was called in to add to the set (and expenses), Edmund found out that Tom was inviting anyone and everyone to the play, even when he'd promised he wouldn't, and now Tom knew all his lines, he was annoyed about the carpenter taking so long to complete his work.

Fanny would listen to everyone's problems (especially Mr Yates, who was disappointed in Henry, thought that Tom spoke too quick, that Mrs Grant laughed too much, Edmund was behind with learning his lines and Mr Rushworth constantly needed a prompter). Mr Rushworth complained that no one rehearsed with him, while Fanny noticed that Maria and Henry rehearsed their first scene together constantly.

It was generally agreed that Henry Crawford was the best actor. Even Fanny, who couldn't like him as a man, liked watching him act. Maria was also a very good actress. When Fanny watched her and Henry practising together on stage, she thought that perhaps Maria was *too* good an actress.

Mr Rushworth had been watching them too, when he said to Fanny, 'How anyone could call such a small, mean-looking man a fine actor is beyond me!'

With all this, Fanny was busier than ever, but at least only half as miserable as everyone else seemed to be. She was constantly needed, especially by her aunt

Norris, who felt Fanny was never doing enough.

Eventually, Fanny managed to escape to the East Room for a little peace and quiet. It was the day that Edmund and Mary would be rehearsing their first scene together and she was filled with anxiety about it. She wanted to watch them and dreaded it at the same time, when there was a knock on the door.

'Miss Price,' said Mary. 'I've come to ask your help.'

'Me?' asked Fanny.

'I need help rehearsing my scene with Mr Edmund Bertram. I've read over it, and . . . well . . . *how* am I to say these things to *him*?'

She handed the book to Fanny, who had already read the lines and knew it was an intimate scene.

'Wouldn't you feel embarrassed?' asked Mary. 'But then, you're his cousin so it wouldn't matter.'

Fanny had no choice. Mary said her lines as Fanny read Edmund's – or Anhalt's – as well as she could. Ten minutes later, there was another knock on the door, before Edmund walked in. All three started in surprise. He had come looking for Fanny for the same reason that Mary had. This was amusing to everyone except Fanny, who they begged to stay to help them. Poor, trapped Fanny.

That evening the first full rehearsal took place. Mary and Henry returned to Mansfield after dinner at the parsonage, but without Mrs Grant, much to the dismay of the other actors.

'Dr Grant needed our sister to stay at home because apparently the pheasant he ate today has given him a bad stomach,' said Mary with a raise of the brow.

'Fanny!' exclaimed Tom. 'You have to fill in.'

Fanny *knew* she should've stayed in her room. Why was she there, anyway? Watching Edmund and Mary act together was only going to make her miserable, and now being forced to act was her punishment.

'You can just sit and read it,' Edmund said, kindly.

While everyone bustled about, getting ready for their performance, Fanny's heart thudded, thinking of Edmund and Mary together, her having to read in front of everyone . . . it was *too* much. Just then, Julia came bursting in, her face flushed.

'Everyone!'

They all turned, startled.

'Father is here!' she exclaimed.

Sir Thomas Bertram had finally returned home.

CHAPTER TWELVE

There was a terrible pause. Each person felt the inconvenience of his return, and as if they had been caught doing something *very* wrong. Even Julia managed to feel sorry for everyone. Until she saw Henry's hand in Maria's.

'At least *I* am in the clear,' she added as she swept out of the room.

Her movement inspired everyone else to move. Tom and Edmund went to meet their father, followed by Maria. Any doubts Maria had about Henry's feelings were put to rest when he'd held on to her hand. Her father was nothing – she was ready to face anything.

'What about me? Shall I come too?' asked Mr Rushworth, as the three left the room, ignoring him. 'Should I go?'

'Yes, yes, you must,' replied Henry, and Mr Rushworth ran off after the Bertrams.

Fanny was left behind with Mr Yates and the Crawfords. She remembered how much her uncle scared her and now it was coupled with anxiety about Edmund (and the rest of them). The Crawfords and Mr Yates were allowed to be as annoyed as they wanted now.

'I suppose I'd better go to him,' said Fanny, almost to herself.

'Yes, you must,' answered Mary. 'We'll leave the family to reunite. Mr Yates, you're welcome to join us at the parsonage.'

'No need,' he replied, not thinking that Sir Thomas would want to be alone with his family after such a long time away from home. 'I'll stay and say hello, as is decent.'

Fanny sighed and left. She approached the door
behind which the Bertrams and Mrs Norris had all
gathered, and entered just to hear Sir Bertram say
'Where is my dear Fanny?'

He gave her such an affectionate hug and kiss
that she felt bad for finding him so intimidating.

'How are you, my dear girl? Well, you don't have to tell me. You are the picture of health and beauty. How is William? It is so good to see you looking so well.'

Fanny's heart felt full as she looked at her uncle, who was thinner and paler, and who seemed so much softer than she remembered. Lady Bertram was so happy to see her husband, she'd moved her pug off the sofa to make room for him.

Mrs Norris, as usual, was creating a bustle when only peace was required.

'Would you like dinner?' she asked. 'Maybe soup? Fanny, ring the bell for soup!'

'I see nothing has changed,' Sir Bertram replied with good humour. 'Just tea will be fine, when it's ready.'

He looked around him, delighted to be home again.

'Imagine what the young ones have been doing lately?' said Lady Bertram, who was quite in the mood to say a word or two. 'Acting!'

'Indeed?' he said.

'Oh, it's nothing,' Tom hastily added. 'Just something to keep mother and ourselves amused. You'll hear about it soon enough.'

The disaster was delayed as they all took tea, but it wasn't long after that Sir Bertram was ready to look around his house, and especially his billiard room, which is where the play had been set up. Before anyone could do anything, he had walked out of the door in the direction of the stage.

'Mr Yates is still there,' said Fanny in an urgent tone.

Tom rushed off and entered the room to see his father meet Mr Yates. He couldn't help but notice Sir Bertram's surprise at the changes, the stage, the carpenter's voice booming behind it. Sir Bertram looked at Tom with alarm, while trying to remain polite towards Mr Yates, who wouldn't stop talking. Eventually, Sir Bertram returned to the drawing room, where the rest of the family were still waiting. Tom and Mr Yates followed him in.

'I have seen your little theatre,' he said, solemnly.

Mr Yates took this as his cue to explain, in detail, what had happened. He didn't notice the way Sir Bertram looked at his daughters, his gaze resting on Edmund, speaking a thousand words of displeasure. Fanny hated to see it, even though she knew, in her heart, that Edmund was not blameless. Sir Thomas simply bowed his head by the end of Mr Yates's very long speech.

'And that's how we came to act, Father,' added Tom.

'It'd be excellent to have your audience tomorrow when we start rehearsals again,' said Mr Yates.

'You shall have my audience,' said Sir Bertram seriously. 'But without any rehearsal.'

Everyone remained silent until Sir Bertram spoke again. 'I've heard a lot about the Crawfords. Are they nice people?'

'Henry's a great fellow, and Miss Crawford very elegant and lively,' said Tom.

'You should point out to your father that Henry isn't more than five foot eight, or he'll expect someone handsome,' interrupted Mr Rushworth.

Sir Thomas looked at him in surprise.

'I have to say,' added Mr Rushworth. 'I much prefer sitting here, like this, to acting.'

Sir Thomas smiled approvingly. 'I'm happy to find someone your age who thinks so sensibly.'

Mr Rushworth was so pleased with the praise that he was lost for words, and so Sir Thomas was prevented from finding out how stupid Mr Rushworth was for a little longer.

CHAPTER THIRTEEN

The next day, the first thing Edmund did was go to his father to explain everything. He found, however, that all his justifications felt flimsy.

'There's only one person without any kind of blame,' Edmund added. 'And that's Fanny.'

Sir Thomas wanted to forgive Edmund, so shook his hand. Once the house was its usual self he didn't even want to speak to any of the others about it, feeling that they'd be sorry enough. He certainly tried not to think of how they'd forgotten him.

The only person to whom he wanted to show his disapproval was Mrs Norris.

'I thought you might have told the children why it was wrong,' he said to her.

She was so surprised that she was *almost* silent for the first time in her life.

'I . . . It . . .'

She couldn't admit, though, that she hadn't seen why it was wrong, nor that even if she had, no one would've listened to her. She did the only thing she could do, and that was change the subject.

'I've saved the household much expense since you've been away, and was so busy ensuring Maria and Mr Rushworth's engagement went smoothly that, well . . . I can't keep tabs on *everything*.'

'Well,' said Sir Thomas, giving up. 'I didn't find anything remarkable about him, but at least he preferred family time to acting.'

'The more you know him, the better he is,' said Mrs Norris, listing at length his somewhat mediocre qualities, as Sir Thomas listened politely while thinking of all the things he had to get done.

This included, most importantly, the removal of *all* signs of *Lovers' Vows*. Poor Mr Yates had to take a second blow to his acting career. He would've told everyone how he felt about Sir Thomas' unreasonable behaviour if it weren't for Julia. Instead, he remained quiet and stayed an extra few days at Mansfield Park. Sir Thomas could thank Julia for that.

Maria was perhaps the most agitated. She expected Henry to declare his love any minute. Mr Rushworth had gone back to Sotherton and with any luck, he'd never come back. Except, there'd been no word from the Crawfords. It was the first time since they had arrived that the families had gone twenty-four hours without seeing one another.

The following day promised to be as gloomy, until Dr Grant and Henry came to pay their respects to Sir Thomas. Maria's heart fluttered with expectation. After some polite conversation, Henry said, 'Will the play continue? I'm called away for business by my uncle, but I'll delay it if I'm wanted here. Nothing's more important than what we began.'

Maria's heart sank. Tom assured Henry there would be *no* play.

'I'm sorry to hear it,' replied Henry. 'So I must go.'

Maria steadied herself. She knew Henry well enough to know that if he had wanted to, he would stay. Her hands trembled, but she had enough pride to seem unbothered. The visit to say hello became the visit to say goodbye for Henry, and so ended his selfish ways that inspired Maria and Julia to love him. Julia was glad he was gone, and now that he wasn't going to marry Maria, she could even feel sorry for her sister.

The unbearable John Yates left a few days later,

much to Sir Thomas's relief, especially given how attentive he was towards Julia. Mrs Norris was obviously upset that nothing became of Henry and Julia. But she made herself feel better by reminding herself that she couldn't think of *everyone*.

Mansfield Park was now all gloom. The only people Sir Thomas liked to have over were the Rushworths. The Grants and the Crawfords were ignored, and Edmund felt the lack of it.

'They were so good to Mother while Father was away,' said Edmund to Fanny one day. 'I wish he'd give them more attention. We need some liveliness,' he added. 'Tom's restless, and my sisters are irritable . . . Everything feels so changed.'

'Really?' answered Fanny. 'The evenings now seem just like they were before Uncle left. We were never that lively.'

Edmund thought about this. 'You're right.

Only, after such a short time in the Crawfords' company it felt as if we'd never lived any other way.'

'The quiet suits me very well. I suppose I'm different to everyone.'

Edmund smiled. '*Suppose*? Fanny, if you're looking for compliments then you should go to your uncle. Father thinks you've grown into a very fine woman, I'm afraid. You will have to make your peace with the fact that you are very pretty.'

'Please, stop!' exclaimed Fanny, overcome with embarrassment.

'Your uncle has a high opinion of you,' said Edmund. 'You should talk to him more.'

'I thought I was . . . Although, I don't like asking him too many questions, because what if he feels his own daughters should be asking them?'

'Miss Crawford was right about you. We talked about you at the parsonage the other day.

She said that you are as afraid of being praised as most women are of being neglected. She's remarkable at reading people. I wish Father could meet her.'

Fanny felt that she should be gracious towards Mary and so simply replied, 'Once he's had time with his family, I think everything will return to normal. Anyway, tomorrow the men are all to dine at Sotherton, aren't they?'

Edmund sighed. 'Yes. It will be an evening of stupidity. After a few hours in Mr Rushworth's company, Father will no longer be able to lie to himself about his character. I wish he and Maria had never met.'

In fact, Sir Thomas had already become aware of how silly Mr Rushworth was. He had wanted a better son-in-law, but was more concerned about Maria. He noticed that she spoke to Mr Rushworth without any affection. Financially, it would be a very good marriage, and Sir Thomas was aware that they had been engaged a long time now, but he did not desire his daughter's happiness to be sacrificed.

With all the kindness of a father, he asked about her feelings, for her to be honest with him and that if she were unhappy, he would break up the engagement. Maria struggled for a moment, but she would not give Henry the satisfaction. Plus, she needed her independence from her father. So, not only did she say that she believed her marriage would be a happy one, but that she wanted the wedding to take place at once. Mr Rushworth couldn't have been more delighted, and Sir Thomas couldn't have been more relieved.

Within a month, the wedding took place. Maria looked elegant and beautiful, her father gave her away, her mother stood with smelling salts in her hands, expecting to be overwhelmed, and her aunt Norris tried to cry.

⋆ MANSFIELD PARK ⋆

Once married, she and Mr Rushworth went to
Brighton before going on to London, and Julia went
with them to their new town house. The sisters had
made up after the Henry episode. Julia could do
with the entertainment, and Maria, unfortunately,
needed a companion other than her husband.

CHAPTER FOURTEEN

Tom had gone to London again (to throw away more of his – and Edmund's – inheritance money), and with the sisters also absent, Fanny's importance in the household increased. She was now needed for more than errands. She had even become a regular visitor at the parsonage – much to the delight of Mrs Grant (who worried her sister would get bored) and Mary, who liked nothing more than to entertain. It was a strange friendship. Fanny was restless until she had visited, and yet when she did, she couldn't agree with Mary about the things they talked about, let alone love her as a friend ought to.

One day, they were sitting in the shrubbery and Fanny couldn't help but exclaim, 'To think, this was nothing a few years ago and Mrs Grant has changed it entirely. Nature amazes me.'

'Mmmm,' said Mary, not paying attention. 'If someone had told me that I'd be spending month after month *here,* in a village, when I'm so used to London parties and social gatherings, I'd never have believed them. It's been the quietest five months I've ever known.'

'Too quiet for you, I suppose?'

'In *theory*.' Mary paused. 'But it's also been the happiest summer I've ever known.' She looked thoughtful and Fanny's heartbeat quickened. 'I don't know what it might lead to, but living in such a place doesn't feel as bad as I thought it would.'

When the two looked up, they saw Edmund and Mrs Grant walking towards them. It was the first time Edmund had seen the two together since knowing of their growing friendship and it couldn't have pleased him more. He knew that Fanny was not the only one to gain something by being Mary's friend.

'The turkey will be wasted for this Sunday,' said Mrs Grant, with a sigh.

'What problems you married people have in the countryside!' exclaimed Mary.

'Believe me, you'll have just as many problems in town. Especially with the expense of things.'

Mary laughed. 'I'll be too rich to worry about money. Being rich is the best recipe for happiness.'

'You want to be *very* rich?' asked Edmund, looking worried.

'Don't we all?' said Mary.

'I just intend not to be poor,' answered Edmund. 'Isn't that enough?'

'I prefer a life of distinction.'

'Ah,' he replied. 'How might I rise to distinction?'

'You should've joined the army,' said Mary.

'It's too late for that now,' he replied. 'But there are *some* things I'd be very miserable without – they're of a different nature to money, though.'

He said this with so much meaning that both he and Mary seemed self-conscious. Poor Fanny! She watched it all with a pain in her chest. It was lucky the clock had struck three o'clock and she had been away long enough to say that she must leave.

'I came to say that Mother needed you, Fanny. I shall head home with you.'

'Do both come for lunch tomorrow,' said Mrs Grant.

Fanny wasn't used to this attention and didn't know how to reply, so Edmund accepted for both of them. That was, until they got home.

'But I cannot spare Fanny,' said Lady Bertram. 'I will need her to fetch my tea. You don't want to go, do you, Fanny?'

Fanny's heart sank.

'If you ask her like that, of course she'll say no,' said Edmund.

Just then, Sir Thomas came through the door.

'Dear husband, tell me,' said Lady Bertram. 'Can I spare Fanny?'

Edmund filled his father in about the lunch invitation.

'Of course, she should go,' Sir Thomas replied. 'I'm surprised she hasn't been asked before!'

Lady Bertram was satisfied, but the following day, Mrs Norris was in a very bad mood. 'I hope you're very grateful for this, Fanny. But you must remember Mrs Grant's invitation was given only out of respect for your aunt, *not you*.'

Imagine Mrs Norris's astonishment when Sir Thomas came and asked Fanny what time she should like the carriage.

'The carriage?' exclaimed Mrs Norris. 'She can *walk*.'

Fanny, who felt she deserved even less than Mrs Norris thought she did, was embarrassed.

'My niece, *walk* to a dinner engagement! Never,' said Sir Thomas.

The carriage would be ready for her, and that was the end of that.

When Edmund came down (Fanny was scared of being late and was already waiting) he couldn't help but admire his cousin.

'You look very well,' he said, smiling at her.

'It's the new dress that Uncle gave me on Maria's marriage. It's not too much, is it?'

'A white dress could never look too much. I believe Miss Crawford has something similar.'

When they got to the parsonage, they saw another carriage and recognised it as Henry Crawford's.

'This is a wonderful surprise,' said Edmund.

Fanny wished she could feel the same, but she felt Henry had used her cousins too badly to welcome his company. However, there seemed to be so much to discuss that Fanny didn't have to take part in too much conversation. Soon after lunch, they went to the drawing room; Edmund was busy talking to Dr Grant, so Henry was able to corner Fanny and said, 'So, Mr Rushworth is married! Lucky man. Though he must still be distressed about not being able to perform his forty-two lines.'

In that moment, Fanny hated Henry. She couldn't believe how he could speak so carelessly about Maria and Julia, as if nothing had happened.

'His wife's too good for him,' added Henry. 'And *you*,' he said, looking at Fanny. 'You were a very patient friend to Mr Rushworth during our theatrics.'

Fanny felt the blood rush to her face.

'I miss those days. I was never happier,' he said.

'Never happier than when being dishonourable!' Fanny muttered to herself.

Henry seemed not to hear her, and lowered his voice to say, 'If only Sir Thomas's return had been delayed a little longer.'

'My uncle came at *precisely* the right time.'

Fanny had never spoken so much or so angrily to him (or anyone!) and felt her face flush. Henry paused.

'Yes, you're right. We'd got very noisy.'

He tried to talk to her again, but she seemed too unwilling. Mary, in the meantime, was looking at Dr Grant and Edmund.

'What do you think they're talking about?' she said.

'Money, of course,' replied Henry. 'And how Edmund could make more when he takes over the parsonage. He'll have seven hundred a year, which isn't bad.'

Mary scoffed. 'That's easy for someone with as much money as you to say.'

Mary took up her harp. She was annoyed that Edmund *still* wanted to be a clergyman, knowing how she felt about it, which showed that he didn't love her. Well, if he could control how he felt about her, then she could do it just as well.

CHAPTER FIFTEEN

Henry Crawford decided to stay at Mansfield Park for another few weeks.

'How do you think I'm going to amuse myself?' he asked Mary.

'Riding and walking with me, of course.'

'Yes, obviously, and that's wonderful for the body, but what about the *mind*? No, I'm going to make Fanny Price love me!'

Mary laughed out loud. 'Fanny Price! Weren't her cousins enough?'

'She's turned from average looking to *very* pretty. Her manner, the way she carries herself – it's all improved greatly. Yet, I don't understand her. I tried to get her to talk to me but she was determined to dislike me. So, I'm going to *make* her like me.'

'Oh,' replied Mary. 'She's hurt your ego, so that's your attraction to her. Leave her alone. I won't have you harm her. A little love is okay – it might do her good – but not too much, understood?'

'Of course– just enough that she can't wait to see me, loves everything I say, agrees with me about everything and cries whenever I leave her.'

Mary shook her head and sighed, leaving Fanny to her fate.

So, Henry began his pursuit. He knew how much Fanny's brother meant to her and tried to find out when William would be on leave so he could give Fanny the good news. Unfortunately, William had already written to tell her he would, after seven years of absence, be visiting. Fanny was so happy when she told Henry, she forgot all her shyness and dislike and even thanked him for his efforts. This, he felt, was a promising start to his quest for her heart.

Every day, Fanny waited for William, until finally she heard footsteps in the hallway that could only belong to him. She rushed towards him and they hugged (while she cried a little) long enough to give proper respect to so many years of separation.

Mrs Norris was stopped from calling for Fanny, so they could share this moment for as long as they needed.

Sir Thomas eventually greeted William and was very pleased with his kind face and friendly manners. It didn't take long for the brother and sister to speak with complete openness to one another. William shared all his hopes and fears with Fanny, and he listened to her about life at Mansfield Park. Everyone admired how much the brother and sister loved one another. Fanny's allure increased to Henry; she had so much feeling and loyalty without a hint of showing off. He felt that it would be something to be loved by such a girl.

Henry, along with everyone, listened to William's stories of travel and horror and had such respect for him that Henry offered to lend him his horse. Fanny looked at Henry with surprise, but was grateful for the attention he paid her brother.

Henry's stay at Mansfield Park went from two

weeks to being indefinite.

The meeting between the two families was again how it used to be. Sir Thomas began to notice that Henry paid particular attention to Fanny, and believed that he greatly admired her. One evening at the parsonage, after a pleasant dinner, two game tables were set up for *Whist* and *Speculation*.

'Which should I enjoy more?' Lady Bertram asked Sir Thomas.

'*Speculation*, dear,' he answered, for he was to play *Whist*.

Henry settled himself between Fanny and Lady Bertram – as neither knew how to play – with Edmund, Mary and William.

'I forgot to say, after our riding session today, I passed through Thornton Lacey,' said Henry to Edmund.

'How did you find it?'

Mary listened especially carefully, for she knew

this was to be Edmund's home, since Dr and Mrs Grant were at the parsonage, when he became a clergyman.

'You're lucky. It'll only take five years before the farm is useful.'

'It's not that bad,' replied Edmund.

Henry went into detail about what changes would be needed to make the place worth living in.

'I have one or two more ideas about the stream,' added Henry after barely taking a breath.

Edmund laughed. 'Yes, I have one or two myself. I plan to keep it mostly as it is. It will do for me, and all who care about me.'

Mary had been listening as she beat William in their game. She resented the way Edmund's tone had changed, the way he only half-looked at her now, as if his feelings for her had changed.

'Seriously, Bertram,' Henry continued. 'If you

changed it enough, it would be a place of distinction and could earn a good deal of income for you. Don't you agree, Miss Price?'

Fanny shook her head, pretending not to be listening. 'I've not seen it.'

'Mr Bertram,' said Mary, laughingly, since Henry had been too busy flirting with Maria to offer any helpful advice to Mr Rushworth. 'You see what my brother did with Sotherton.'

Fanny looked at Henry, remembering his behaviour to her cousins that day. Henry caught her eye and cleared his throat.

'Oh, I didn't do anything. It was such a hot day; we were all bothered. I believe I have changed since then.'

Henry began talking about getting a place near Thornton Lacey himself, he loved it so much at Mansfield Park. Sir Thomas looked over at their table and noticed how calmly Fanny behaved.

'I hope you'd like me as your neighbour,' said

Henry, realising that Sir Thomas was listening.

'Of course,' Sir Thomas replied. 'It's only right that Edmund should take his place in Thornton Lacey – though I hate the idea of him not being at Mansfield Park any more. In any case, wherever Edmund stays, he will be a fine clergyman. I believe it's his true calling.'

Edmund bowed his head at his father, appreciating his comment.

Fanny was overwhelmed at the idea that there would soon come a time when she would not see Edmund every day. Mary listened with all the dislike of a woman who felt a man – in this case Sir Thomas – was ruining any chance that Edmund might have of changing his mind about joining the clergy. She soon brought the game with William to an end, for she had to keep her spirits up.

Everyone got up and sat or stood around the fire, apart from William and Fanny, who remained at their game table, talking. Henry turned his chair towards them to observe them. He in turn was being observed by Sir Thomas.

'Do you wish you were back at Portsmouth?' Fanny asked William.

'Not at all,' he replied. 'The dances there are wonderful but what's the point when no one wants to dance with me? The ladies only look at lieutenants.'

Fanny's face burned. 'They don't know what they're missing! And one day you *will* be a lieutenant.'

'Maybe,' he replied. 'But it feels like everyone gets ahead but me – I just don't have the superior connections other men do.'

'I'm sure it'll happen one day.'

William smiled. 'I'd love to go to a ball with you. Remember how much fun we'd have as children when we used to dance?'

Fanny took her brother's hand and squeezed it.

'Is Fanny a wonderful dancer?' William said, turning to Sir Thomas.

Fanny was embarrassed by the question and tried to look anywhere but at the faces now observing her.

'I'm afraid I've never seen her. Maybe we'll all get to sooner than we imagined,' Sir Thomas replied.

Henry Crawford leaned forward. 'I've had the pleasure of seeing your sister dance and would be happy to answer any questions you have about it. But not now,' he added, looking at Fanny. 'There's one person here who doesn't like to talk about Miss Price.'

When it was time to leave, Fanny's heart felt full – the evening had been everything she could've asked for. The only disappointment came when Henry put her shawl around her shoulders before Edmund got the chance.

CHAPTER SIXTEEN

The following day, Sir Thomas waited for everyone in the breakfast room, where he announced that he was going to throw a ball at Mansfield Park in Fanny's honour.

'I couldn't have you leave without seeing your sister dance,' he said to William.

'Bu- but . . .' Mrs Norris stuttered. 'Maria and Julia aren't even here!'

Mrs Norris had to calm her feelings, since Sir Thomas had already thought everything through – from the families to invite, right up to the date, which would be two days before William was to leave. He hadn't even consulted her!

Invitations were sent out and during the next few days there was much rushing around, while Lady Bertram lay on the sofa with her pug, hardly noticing.

Edmund was the only one whose thoughts were focused on something aside from the ball: taking ordination, to officially become a clergyman, and getting married. The ordination would take place over Christmas, but getting married was another matter. He knew he wanted Mary as his wife and most of the time he believed that *she* wanted *him* as her husband. He knew she cared about him, but did she care enough to give up her preference for a London lifestyle? His answer always fell between 'yes' and 'no', changing daily, and his stomach was in a state of knots over it.

Mary was to leave Mansfield Park in January to go to London to stay with a friend, and Henry would go with her. The only thing that gave

Edmund any pleasure about the ball was that he would ask her for the first two dances.

Fanny, meanwhile, had no idea what to wear. Specifically, she was worrying about how to wear the amber cross William had given her as a present, since she had no chain to go with it (he couldn't afford the gold one he wanted). She felt she ought not tie it with ribbon for a ball, though that's how she had been wearing it. She decided to go to the parsonage and ask Mrs Grant and Mary for advice, since they both had good taste.

'Don't worry,' said Mary, once Fanny had explained everything. 'We will sort everything.'

Mary got out a little box of trinkets. 'Please take one of these chains and consider it a present.'

'I couldn't,' said Fanny, horrified at such generosity.

'I have so many I'll never wear them all. It's hardly a gift at all. I'm sorry that I'm being so forward but you must humour me.'

Fanny, upon being pressed, felt she *had* to take the present or she'd seem ungrateful.

'I'll think of you and your kindness whenever I wear it,' said Fanny.

'Well, you can think of me *and* Henry. He's the one who gave it to me.'

Fanny was astonished and immediately gave the necklace back. 'I can't take something that was a present – and from your brother too.'

Mary laughed. 'My dear, please don't worry. He's always buying me things. And I'm sure he'd love to see it around such a pretty neck. Unless you think I'm giving it because *he* wants you to have it?'

Fanny's cheeks burned.

'Say no more, please,' said Mary. 'Such a small thing isn't worth half the words we've used to talk about it.'

Poor Fanny was silenced into taking the necklace. She was not stupid. She saw the way Henry talked to her now: like he once had with

Maria and Julia. She supposed he wanted to take away her peace of mind as well, but Fanny knew better than to be taken in by him.

Fanny returned to Mansfield Park and went directly towards her room, ready to put the necklace away. She was caught by surprise at the sight of Edmund at her writing desk. All her agitated feelings disappeared.

'I was just writing you a note,' said Edmund. 'I'm in a rush, but now you're here . . .' he handed her a small package. 'It's a necklace for the cross that William got you.'

Fanny almost burst into tears as she opened the package. Edmund smiled and was about to leave. He seemed in a rush.

'No, wait,' she exclaimed. She looked at the necklace. It was exactly what she had wanted. 'It's the most wonderful thing . . . how can I thank you . . .?'

'Nothing means more to me than bringing you happiness, dear Fanny. But if all you want to do is tell me how much you love it, then you must let me go.'

'Yes, but no . . . there's more.'

She explained how she had received *another* necklace and asked what she should do about it. Edmund was so taken by Mary's kindness that it took him a while to properly understand Fanny's dilemma. It was a few minutes later, by which time Fanny's warm feelings towards Mary had almost disappeared, when Edmund said, 'You can't give it back. It would be painful to her. And anyway, it is much prettier than mine.'

'No, it isn't,' said Fanny.

'You must wear her gift to the ball tomorrow,' said Edmund, with all his usual warmth. 'Keep mine for everyday wear. I couldn't bear it if she misunderstood you.' He paused. 'I wouldn't want to see any kind of coolness between the two of you . . . you are the two *dearest* people to me in the world.'

And with that, he left.

Fanny had to sit down. *She* was one of the dearest people to *Edmund*. But the other . . . Edmund had never been so open, and though Fanny was already sure of how he felt about Mary, now there was no doubt. He *would* marry Mary. Fanny felt such a stab of misery. It wouldn't be so bad if Mary *deserved* Edmund, but Fanny truly felt that her faults were the same as they ever had been, only, he no longer saw them.

On the day of the ball, Henry sent a note to William to ask whether he would like to join him on his upcoming trip to London. William was due to be leaving that day anyway, and Henry invited him to dine with him and his uncle. Although this meant that Fanny would lose half a day with William, she was so happy that William was given the honour of

Henry's uncle's attention, who had such a high standing in society, that her spirits improved.

Knowing that her brother would soon be gone again, the ball no longer seemed exciting to her. She was trudging up the stairs when Edmund appeared.

'Fanny, you must lend me your ear a moment,' he said, seeming a little uneasy. 'You might already know why I have just been to the parsonage. It was to engage Miss Crawford . . .'

Fanny thought she might be sick.

'. . . in the first two dances,' he added. 'I never know how seriously to take her, but she said yes, only that it'll be the last time she dances with me, because she never dances with clergymen. I think she was joking, but I didn't like it. I know she doesn't *mean* to say hurtful things, and she is playful, but . . .'

Fanny hesitated. 'I'm happy to listen to your fears and worries, but please don't ask me for advice. I'm not qualified to give it.'

'Sorry, Fanny, you're right. It's not fair on you – just talking to you helps.'

He took her hand with such affection and love – as if it was Mary Crawford's itself!

'The more I think about it, the more I think my chances are less and less. I worry that it's not just *what* she says that is wrong sometimes, but how she *thinks*. You and I have spoken about it before. I must try to see clearly. Oh, Fanny. You have always been such a dear friend to me.'

He squeezed her hand again and Fanny's heart felt lighter.

Edmund left so that Fanny could get ready. She looked at herself in the mirror and was pleased with the outcome. When it came to the necklace it seemed as if it would be a great day, after all, for the cross wouldn't fit on the chain that Mary had given her. Fanny *had* to wear Edmund's chain with William's cross – *her* two dearest people, now closest to her heart. To make sure that Mary would not be offended, Fanny wore her necklace too. All looked very well to Fanny, who left her room only to find that Lady Bertram had sent her maid to help Fanny get dressed. Of course, it was too late, but Fanny felt her aunt's attention and was very grateful for it.

CHAPTER SEVENTEEN

Sir Thomas told Fanny she looked well, but it was only when she couldn't hear that he praised her beauty.

'I sent my maid to her,' replied Lady Bertram, by way of explanation.

'Of course she'll look well, with everything you've given her,' exclaimed Mrs Norris.

In fact, everyone looked at Fanny approvingly.

'You must have two dances with me,' said Edmund, as he opened the door for her. 'Any dances you wish, except the first.'

The evening brought its trials, as Fanny was forced to speak to strangers introduced by her uncle when all she wanted was to make the most of her time left with William. Once the familiar faces of the Grants and Crawfords arrived, Fanny relaxed. Mary looked lovely and Fanny couldn't help but look between her and Edmund, until she came face to face with Henry.

'May I have the first two dances?' he asked, glancing at her necklace.

How conflicted she felt! To not have a partner for the first two dances would be mortifying, but to have *him* was almost worse. Especially when he looked at her and her necklace that way. There was nothing for it though – she accepted.

Everyone made their way into the ballroom, where Fanny met with Mary and explained what had happened with the necklace. Mary looked delighted.

'Edmund did that? Of course he did! He is the best of men.'

Mary looked around for him, as if she wanted to tell him what she thought of him immediately.

'Now, Fanny, do you have a partner?' came her uncle's voice.

'I do. Mr Crawford.'

It was just as Sir Thomas had thought.

'Excellent, on your way then to start it off.'

Fanny looked at him, surprised. 'Sorry?'

'You must begin the ball, my dear.'

'But, but . . . Edmund and Miss Crawford are to do that, surely?' Fanny couldn't hide the anxiety in her voice.

There was no way she deserved such an honour! To open a ball, but with Mr Crawford! What would her cousins think? All eyes were on Fanny — and though she felt awkward and unworthy, her manners and modesty were very charming.

'Fanny looks very well,' said Mary to Sir Thomas and Lady Bertram. She couldn't forgive them for making Edmund become a clergyman, but she still wanted them to like her.

'She does,' replied Lady Bertram, 'I sent my maid to her.'

Once the dances were over, Mary approached Fanny. 'Maybe you could tell me why my brother's going to London tomorrow?'

Fanny felt her cheeks flush.

'It's the first time he won't confide in me, but I'm afraid there always comes a time when *someone* begins to mean more to a man than his sister.' Mary added, looking meaningfully at her friend.

'Sorry,' said Fanny. 'But I don't know.'

Mary sighed. 'Ah well, I suppose he's just taking William so he can talk about you.'

Fanny couldn't ignore all the attention Henry was giving her. Mary thought that was why Fanny looked pleased, but nothing could've been further from the truth. Her pleasure was in seeing her brother look so happy and, of course, having two dances with Edmund to look forward to. If anything, Henry's attentions spoiled all this.

'I am worn out being nice to people,' said Edmund when their dance finally came. 'It's so nice to be with you right now, so I can have some peace!'

So they danced in silence. In truth, Edmund was annoyed. Today, Mary's liveliness made him feel worse, not better. She'd said things about his profession that were hurtful and even unkind. They'd argued about it and both left each other upset. Fanny had been watching, and though she hated to see Edmund suffer, she felt this was better for him in the long run.

The night soon came to a close. Even though Fanny was exhausted, she insisted she'd be up in the morning to see William off. No one could persuade her otherwise.

'Mr Crawford, you must also join us for breakfast,' said Sir Thomas.

Mr Crawford was so quick to answer yes that Sir Thomas was now absolutely sure that Henry was in love with Fanny. And, not knowing how Henry had behaved with his daughters, it pleased him very much.

CHAPTER EIGHTEEN

Fanny said goodbye to William and Sir Thomas left her in peace to cry over him, and Henry, the man he assumed she had fallen in love with. Edmund left the same day for Peterborough. Everyone was gone. Fanny had nothing but her memories and no one to share them with. To add to this, Sir Thomas told Lady Bertram that he had agreed for Julia to extend her stay with Maria in London.

'I wish everyone would stay home to care for their poor mama. I am glad we took Fanny when we did,' replied Lady Bertram. 'And we shall *always* have her.'

'As long as we can before she might go somewhere she might find more happiness.'

'That's not likely,' said Lady Bertram. 'Maria might call her to Sotherton every now and then, but not to *stay*. Anyway, I can't do without her.'

Fanny quickly became used to the quiet house and set about her routine. Mary, on the other hand, felt very hard done by. The winter brought such miserable weather with the rain and snow! She thought about Edmund *all* the time. She missed him more than she wanted and worried she had been rude to him. They had hardly parted as friends and it was her fault. This anxiety only got worse when she heard that his week-long trip would be extended because he'd be staying with a friend. Then she was struck by something she'd never felt before: jealousy. His friend was sure to have sisters — were they attractive? Why did he stay away when he *knew* that she would be leaving for London soon? It was too much. Mary would brave the snow to see Fanny and get some answers.

After some small talk about the weather, Mary said, 'You must miss Edmund. Aren't you surprised that he's stayed away so long?'

'I suppose,' replied Fanny.

'I'd wanted to see him before I left, to say goodbye properly. Would you say goodbye from me? Give him my . . . compliments? That feels cold, doesn't it? Considering how much time we've spent together. There should be a word, something between compliments and – love? – yes. Compliments will have to do. Do you know how many sisters his friend has?'

'Mr Owen? Three, I think.'

'Are they musical?' Mary asked, trying to sound like she didn't care.

'I don't know.'

Mary paused. 'I hate to leave. Mrs Grant doesn't want me to go. Edmund will find Mansfield Park very quiet with all the loud ones gone!'

Fanny felt she had to speak. 'You'll be missed by everyone.'

'Oh, I'm not fishing for compliments,' said Mary, wanting Fanny to say more. 'And anyone who wants to see me will know how to reach me,' she added.

Fanny smiled.

'One of the Miss Owens might end up marrying Mr Bertram,' said Mary, laughingly. 'Everyone wants to marry well, and a Miss Owen *should* if she marries someone like Edmund. Don't you expect it?'

'Not at all,' said Fanny.

'Not at all!' cried Mary. 'I do wonder – but then you know him better than most . . .'

And, catching Fanny blush, Mary felt her spirits lift and changed the subject.

Mary's spirits lifted further when Henry returned

that evening. He still hadn't told her why he'd gone to London, but she wasn't annoyed about it – it had all become quite humorous. The following day, Henry went to pay his respects to the Bertrams and told Mary he would return in ten minutes for their walk. An hour and a half later, he finally appeared back at the parsonage.

'I couldn't leave,' he said apologetically, as he gave her his arm. 'I was with Fanny and Lady Bertram.'

'Why did you suffer that for so long?' exclaimed Mary.

Henry looked at his sister. 'I couldn't leave Fanny. Mary, I must tell you that I'm genuinely in love with Fanny Price and mean to make her my wife.'

Mary thought he was joking.

'She's the most perfect creature. I know, I know, I had other ideas when it all began, but I've discovered that she's one of the finest ladies I've *ever* met,' said Henry.

'My God! You're actually serious.'

'I am.'

It took a few moments for Mary to absorb all of this, but once she did, she realised how happy it made her.

'It's the perfect match! I never would've thought of it, but she's a dear, gentle soul and will make you a very good wife. That *lucky* girl! The more I think of it, the more I love the idea.'

Because the more Mary thought of it, the more she realised how close *her* family would become to the Bertrams.

'And you're richer than her, so she'll be even more grateful for your love,' added Mary. 'Mrs Norris will chew her hand off. What are you waiting for, then?'

'I just need the opportunity. She's not like her cousins and I'm not so sure of her feelings, but I don't think she'll say no.'

'*No?*' cried Mary. 'To a man like you? Even if she *doesn't* love you right now, she's such a sweet girl she'd feel awful, and will make herself love you.'

Henry had been listening to his sister with all the hope and joy of a man in love.

'And how will the Bertram sisters take it?' asked Mary.

'I don't care! They could learn a thing or two

from Fanny. The way she's been treated by everyone in that family is abominable.'

'Aside from Edmund,' interrupted Mary. 'And her uncle has been good.'

'Oh, yes, aside from Edmund, I suppose. Her uncle gives her all the cold affection only an uncle can. Anyway, whatever affection *they* might've given her, it won't compare one bit to mine.'

CHAPTER NINETEEN

When the precious letter Henry had been waiting for arrived, he didn't waste a minute in rushing to take it to Mansfield Park. The moment he had the chance, he handed it to Fanny.

'I've been impatient to give this to you, but I had to wait until it was confirmed and now it is.'

Fanny looked at him, confused, not reading the letter, but rather the expression on his face.

'Your brother, William . . . he's been made a lieutenant.'

Fanny was lost for words. She skimmed over the letter, too confused to take it all in, but read enough to know that Henry was telling the truth.

'After my uncle met William, he wanted nothing more than to make sure he got promoted.'

Fanny looked up at Henry. 'You and your uncle made this happen?'

Henry nodded and was delighted to explain everything.

'It's the reason I took William to London. I told no one about it until it was all done. Not even Mary.'

'Oh, you are so kind!' exclaimed Fanny. 'I'm so grateful to you. I have to tell my uncle.'

She was already at the door, about to leave, when Henry took her hand and sat her back down. He began to tell her that he had done this out of love for *her*. How could Fanny utter how she felt? She was full of joy for her brother, but so insulted that Henry Crawford should speak to her in the same way he had probably spoken to Maria and Julia.

'Please, Mr Crawford, you mustn't talk this way. I don't like it.'

But he kept telling her how strongly he felt, and then, much to Fanny's confusion, he offered her his hand in marriage. He couldn't be serious! Fanny couldn't speak.

'Will you make me the happiest man alive?'

'No, no, no! I thank you from my heart for your kindness to William, but you're *not* thinking of me. I know it's all nothing.'

Just then, they heard Sir Thomas's voice speaking to the servant outside and Fanny burst away from Henry, towards another door, leaving the room just as her uncle entered it.

She paced up and down the East Room, unable to sit still. She felt joy for William but such horror for herself. Henry wouldn't address her again – not after how she reacted. But if he stopped this nonsense, perhaps she could be good friends with him.

Fanny heard him leave and rushed to her uncle, for she wanted to share the news about William. Sir Thomas was very pleased and told her that he'd asked Henry back to have dinner with them that evening.

This was awful. She tried to seem normal but when Henry appeared that evening she was desperately uncomfortable until he walked up to her and handed her a letter from Mary.

> *My dear Fanny,*
>
> *I had to offer my congratulations. I am delighted to give all my love and consent on the matter and promise there will be no difficulties. Now go and smile your sweetest of smiles to my brother, who will come back home even happier than when he left.*

Fanny didn't know what to think. Was Henry *serious*? She wasn't sure which was worse. She couldn't eat, and only waited for the whole thing to be over. At last, they retired to the drawing room. How could a man who had flirted with so many before, with women far better than Fanny, be in love with *her*? It must be a joke. Only when Sir Thomas and Henry walked into the room, she saw that Henry *did* look serious. A very long time seemed to pass before Henry decided to leave. He took her hand, looked at her meaningfully and whispered, 'My dear wife-to-be.'

Fanny woke up just as distressed as when she'd gone to sleep. This was only made worse when she saw Henry walking towards the house from her window. She would *not* go downstairs unless she was called. Half an hour had passed and Fanny was just getting comfortable, when she heard footsteps – the same ones that filled her with fear when she was growing up. There was a knock on her door.

'Uncle,' she said, as Sir Thomas walked in.

Fanny began making a fuss and getting him a chair when he said, 'You have no fire in here! It's snowing outside and you're just wearing a shawl. How is this possible?'

Poor Fanny was forced to mumble something about Mrs Norris saying it wasn't necessary.

'I see. She takes things too far with you

sometimes, Fanny, but I hope you will always respect her. I know you are too generous not to.'

Fanny could only give a weak smile.

'Anyway, I'm here because I've just been visited by Mr Crawford. I think you know why.'

He smiled warmly and it made her feel sick as he told her how Henry had come to declare himself in love with Fanny and ask her uncle for her hand in marriage.

'He has been a complete gentleman, my dear girl, and now I come to tell you that he is still here and wishes to see you before he leaves.'

'No!' Fanny exclaimed, shocking herself and her uncle.

'No?'

'I don't *want* to see him.'

'What do you mean?' Sir Thomas asked. 'He said that you felt the same.'

'No, Uncle, that's not true. I made it very clear . . . I mean, I *think* . . . I'm *sure*. I told him I didn't like hearing such things and that he must stop.'

Her uncle had to pause for a few moments. 'Are you telling me that you don't want to marry Mr Crawford?'

'Absolutely not,' she said.

'You're *refusing* him?'

Fanny nodded. 'Yes, sir.'

Sir Thomas couldn't help but be astonished. 'But *why*? He's someone you've known for months, he's been a friend of the family, his sister is a good friend of yours, he is charming and well-liked, he has money – everything about him makes him a good match. Beyond all that, think of what he's done for your brother . . . is there any reason you might think badly of Mr Crawford?'

What could Fanny say? How was she to explain it to him without bringing down her cousins?

'No, sir.'

'And you *still* mean to refuse him?'

She nodded. There was a long, terrifying pause.

'Fanny, I cannot tell you how disappointed I am in you. *You*, who I thought so well of when I came back from Antigua, have turned out to be the most selfish, ungrateful girl I know. If he was half the man he is now I'd have been glad for him to marry Julia, and *you*?'

Fanny was sobbing by now. To be accused of being such things in such a cold manner broke her heart. Sir Thomas saw how she wept and calmed down a little. Perhaps she just needed some time, he thought. If Henry really loved her, he might persevere. Fanny was in such a state that Sir Thomas felt that if there *were* to be any hope, she had better stay in her room. So, he left his niece in floods of tears. Her mind was in disorder. Her heart was broken over her uncle's harsh words and her one friend was not there to comfort her. Maybe Edmund would see it exactly as her uncle did. Sir

Thomas soon returned to tell her that Henry had left. He was calmer and the coldness in his tone had almost gone.

'He has taken it as you can expect, but insisted that you not be pressed. This just makes him more admirable. But you must see him soon, Fanny. I won't tell anyone about what has passed for now. I suggest you go out and get some air. It will do you some good.'

Fanny was relieved. She would rather have to speak to Henry than have to listen to Mrs Norris repeating how ungrateful she was. She took her uncle's advice and went outside to the shrubbery.

When she returned to her room, the fire had been lit. The maid said Sir Thomas had ordered it so every day.

'I *must* be selfish,' she cried to herself.

CHAPTER TWENTY

Henry was so used to getting what he wanted from women that Fanny's resistance only made her more appealing. Little did he know that he was attacking a heart that belonged to someone else. Instead, he was taken by the idea of forcing Fanny to love him, just as Sir Thomas hoped. So, he returned to Mansfield Park that evening.

Fanny was bewildered when he repeated his love for her. She told him she did not love him, never could and never would; that they were the opposite of each other; that everything about it was *unthinkable*. He seemed to be truly in love with her, though, and what's more, she could not forget that he'd got William his promotion. But his stubborn pursuit showed the same ungenerous Henry Crawford who had once played with both her cousins' feelings and who only cared about what he wanted. Even *if* Fanny didn't love another, she felt certain she *still* wouldn't love him.

Henry told Sir Thomas about his conversation (one-sided as it was) with Fanny, and though Sir Thomas was disappointed, he believed that Henry would eventually succeed with someone as gentle as his niece.

'You'll not hear about it from me again,' he said to Fanny. 'I will never force you to marry someone. It is all in Mr Crawford's hands now. In any case, he will be leaving soon.'

This was all she hoped for. Fanny was certain that Mr Crawford's love couldn't last, but she hadn't realised that Henry wanted Sir Thomas to tell Lady Bertram and her sister. There were to be no secrets about his love, and though Sir Thomas would have preferred not tell Mrs Norris, it couldn't be avoided.

Thankfully, Mrs Norris didn't say anything to Fanny, merely gave her angry looks. In fact, she wasn't annoyed that Fanny had rejected Henry, but rather that he had proposed to her in the first place. Especially when she thought of her dear Julia. As for Lady Bertram, she had never been sure whether Fanny was beautiful but was now convinced that she must be.

'I am so happy, my dear!' said Lady Bertram.

'But aren't you glad I said no?' said Fanny, hopefully. 'You need me here, don't you?'

'Not if you married Henry Crawford! He has so much money. And when this kind of offer comes a girl's way, she has a duty to accept it.'

In ten years, this was the only piece of advice her aunt had ever given her.

'I'm sure he fell in love with you the night of the ball,' Lady Bertram added. 'Everyone said how well you looked. I'm so glad I had my servant help you dress. I must tell Sir Thomas that's the night it must've happened.'

CHAPTER TWENTY-ONE

Edmund returned home prepared to be sad about his lost love. But when he saw Henry and Mary arm in arm, walking towards him on his horse, Mary spoke to him with such warmth and good humour that the love didn't feel so lost after all.

When he finally reached home, he was told of William's promotion, which he couldn't have been happier about, and then, speaking to his father alone, he was told about Fanny's promotion in the eyes of Henry. He was surprised at first, but felt that Henry's choice of wife did him credit. He respected and cared for his friend even more as a result of it.

As soon as he came out he sat next to Fanny, took her hand, and squeezed it, trying to show his support. He knew Fanny well enough to know that Henry had gone about it all wrong. Someone like Fanny should not be overwhelmed. He was sure that with time and effort she would love Henry as much as he seemed to love her.

Henry came to dine at Mansfield Park the following day and Edmund observed how Fanny acted around him. He believed that Fanny deserved every bit of love and attention that was shown her, but there was nothing that suggested she wanted any attention. Edmund felt that if he were Henry, he wouldn't have persevered in the same way.

After dinner, the men joined the women in the drawing room. Fanny was hard at work on some embroidery, refusing to look up. Lady Bertram, who everyone always assumed was half-asleep, explained that Fanny had only just put down some Shakespeare before they'd entered.

It wasn't long before Henry took up the book and began reading from it. Fanny seemed determined not to look up, to continue with her needlework, but Henry *was* a very good actor. His reading was possibly the best she had ever heard. It pleased Edmund when she looked up. There might be hope for his friend yet.

'I wish my sermons were as good as your readings,' said Edmund.

'There's such beauty in the language of our religion that sermons can't ever be fully bad, though I confess I can get distracted sometimes. I hope to do better from now on.'

He gave a side glance to Fanny.

Fanny shook her head and of course Henry noticed. He was instantly by her side. Why did she shake her head? Was it what he said about being constant? Edmund removed himself and sat in the chair by the fire, taking up a newspaper. Henry kept asking her and she was forced to respond, 'I– well . . . I just thought it's a shame you have not always known yourself as well as you seem to now,' she replied.

'I will *always* be constant in my feelings for you.'

Fanny blushed, asking him to not speak that way. It was a good thing that the servant came in with tea and cake and Henry was forced to move, or she didn't know what she would have done. Edmund looked at it all, hoping that his friend might have gained some favour with Fanny.

The Crawfords were to have their last dinner at Mansfield Park before they went back to London, which Sir Thomas hoped would sway Fanny into loving Henry. Edmund was surprised that Fanny hadn't come to him about Henry yet. He didn't want to bring it up until she did, except that Sir Thomas had asked him to speak with her.

'You may as well do it now. She's in the shrubbery,' said Sir Thomas.

Edmund felt he had little choice.

'May I join you in your walk?' he asked Fanny.

She nodded. He could tell by her look she was feeling low.

'Fanny, I know there's a lot on your mind, I've heard about it from everyone but you.'

'If you've heard it from everyone, there can't

be much more to tell you.'

'Facts, yes. It's feelings I'm talking about,' he replied.

'We think too differently on this for it to be any comfort to me.'

'We all think Henry's a good match for you, but if you have no love for him, then you were right to refuse him – don't we think the same on that matter?'

She looked up at him, relieved, tears brimming in her eyes. 'I thought you blamed me, like everyone else.'

Edmund smiled. 'You'd have known that's not true if you'd spoken to me. I know you don't care for him now, but his love is not the ordinary kind. He'll carry on like this, and I think, dear Fanny, that you, being the gentle-hearted woman that you are, can't deny him for much longer if he does.'

'I will *never* return his love,' she exclaimed, with much more feeling than she had meant to.

Edmund was surprised. '*Never?*'

'Only that . . . I don't *think* I shall. I am *sure* I think I never shall.'

'I'm sure you don't want to leave Mansfield Park, and that's part of the reason, but don't you *wish* you felt more for him?'

'We're so unlike,' she replied, avoiding answering directly. 'We'd be miserable together.'

'You have similar taste in literature and music and though you're more serious than he is, I think his lively manner will help you see things aren't as difficult as you think they are.'

Fanny had to pause. She knew Edmund was thinking of Mary. He'd not stopped talking about her since he'd got back to Mansfield Park.

'That's not all I meant,' she added, 'although I don't agree with you. I believe he behaved very badly towards Mr Rushworth during the play, and his attentions to Maria weren't proper.'

Edmund hardly listened and merely said, 'Oh,

Fanny, don't judge any of us by what we all did back then. We were *all* in the wrong.'

'And then, there was Julia, who he paid attention to before that,' she added.

'Julia? I never saw anything serious. I think my sisters *wished* for his attention and he's so charming, but I don't feel he did anything wrong. And remember, his uncle wasn't the best influence. How could Henry and Mary be blamed in some of their views, given their upbringing? He'll make you happy, Fanny, but *you*, with your strong principles and gentle character, will make him *everything*.'

'I don't want that responsibility,' exclaimed Fanny.

Edmund shook his head. 'Underestimating yourself, as always. Well, you know enough that for me, after your happiness, his comes next.'

Yes, Fanny knew. They walked a while in silence before Edmund said, 'I was worried Miss

Crawford would think Henry should've chosen a woman with a higher status, but she spoke about you with such affection. It proved to me she is just as kind as I thought. Of course, she says she's angry with you – as angry as any sister who wants the best for her brother would be. Just think if it were William in the same situation . . . Such a man as Henry isn't used to being refused,' Edmund teased.

After some thought, Fanny replied 'Imagine if Henry weren't serious and I ended up liking him just because I *thought* he liked me? A woman shouldn't be expected to love a man just because *he* loves her.'

Edmund almost laughed. 'The way you think shows a superior mind.'

He saw that Fanny looked upset, though, and decided not to mention Henry again, except to tell her that the Crawfords would be leaving on Monday.

'And to think I'd almost stayed away until that

day. I would've regretted it my whole life.'

'Were the Miss Owens nice?'

'Very nice, but I am used to extraordinary women. You and Miss Crawford have ruined me in that.'

CHAPTER TWENTY-TWO

Edmund and Sir Thomas agreed that they'd let things run their course between Henry and Fanny – although Sir Thomas wished Fanny's feelings would hurry up a bit.

Fanny, in the meantime, couldn't bear the idea of facing Mary's wrath for not being in love with her brother, but Mary wasn't a woman easily distracted. She asked to speak with Fanny in private at Mansfield Park. There was nothing Fanny could do but lead Mary up to the East Room.

'Dear girl! What have you done?' Mary exclaimed when they went in.

Fanny had prepared herself for an unpleasant conversation, but Mary was too taken aback by the room and the memories it held. Mary gazed around with a distant look.

'This is where Mr Bertram and I practised our lines for *Lover's Vows* in front of you, remember? That was the happiest week of my life. Then your uncle came and ruined it all.' She laughed. 'No, I know he's a good man, but I wish we could've completed what we set out to do. Look at me, I came here to tell you off but now I'm here, I don't have the heart to do it! I do love you so very much.'

She hugged Fanny so tightly, and it was all said with such genuine warmth that Fanny couldn't help but be affected by it.

'I feel like I'm leaving behind the best of friends,' Mary added. 'My London friends don't hold a candle to all of you. You have to come and visit. When you see how women fall at Henry's feet, your feelings will change. You *must* have noticed his change in attitude and the attention he's showed you, like the necklace.'

Fanny paused. 'You mean the necklace was his idea?'

'Of course!'

'But that is very wrong,' exclaimed Fanny. 'I'd never have taken it if I'd known. As for your brother's attentions – yes, I noticed it, but it didn't mean much since . . . well, he'd paid that kind of attention to both my cousins too. I couldn't take it seriously. It's not right to play with a woman's feelings like that.'

'I did tell him off for that, but you must forgive him. I'm sure you'll tell him off as much as you want when you're married. The truth is, I've never seen him happier. When he got your brother's commission, he was over the moon.'

Fanny heart softened. Mary went on about how difficult it had been getting the Admiral on side but Henry was persistent. He didn't give up and he got his reward.

'I've heard that Mr Edmund Bertram and Sir Thomas will be in London at some point, visiting Julia and Mrs Rushworth, so I'm looking forward to being in their company again, but I will miss you. Will you promise to write to me?' asked Mary.

Fanny had no choice but to say yes.

The meeting was over, much to Fanny's relief. That evening Henry came to say goodbye. He seemed quieter than usual and Fanny felt sorry for him, though she hoped she might not see him again until he was safely someone else's husband.

With Henry gone, Sir Thomas watched Fanny every day, looking for signs of her missing the attention which would flatter even the most modest of women. He found nothing. She had such a calm personality he couldn't detect *what* she was feeling. So, naturally, he asked Edmund.

'It's only been a few days,' replied Edmund.

But Edmund did wonder that Fanny didn't talk more about missing Mary. They'd been such friends! Fanny in turn was sure that when Edmund went to London in a few weeks (he was talking of nothing else) he'd ask Mary to marry him and she'd say yes. Any hesitation they'd both had about each other would be overshadowed by love. And yet, Fanny knew, despite all of Mary's kindness, she was not the right partner for Edmund.

In the meantime, Sir Thomas wouldn't be able to see any change in Fanny because she was too happy that William had ten days' holiday and was coming to see her. What's more, after a talk with Edmund, Sir Thomas decided that Fanny should go to Portsmouth with William and see the rest of her family. But this was less out of affection for his niece and more so that Fanny might understand and appreciate the comfort of the home she was now used to – which would hopefully lead her to appreciate the home that Henry could give her.

If Fanny had ever come close to undisguised joy, it was when her uncle told her that she'd be visiting her family, who she had not seen almost half her life. To know that she'd be amongst them with William for a few months was too much joy to bear. And then to be away from any mention of the Crawfords! And also Edmund. She would not have to see him every day, knowing whose image he carried in his heart. She could just think of him far away in London, which at Mansfield Park might have been unbearable, but at home, with her family and William, would only simply be quite hard.

Lady Bertram took some convincing. She was sure she couldn't do without Fanny, but Mrs Norris soon persuaded her otherwise – telling her she'd be much more use to her sister than Fanny.

'Maybe so, but I think I shall *still* miss her,' said Lady Bertram.

Fanny didn't leave as happily as she thought she would. She cried as she hugged her aunt Bertram, took Sir Thomas's hand and sobbed for letting him down, and could barely look at Edmund.

'Write to me soon, my dear girl,' said Lady Bertram. 'And I shall write to you too.'

Fanny promised she would.

'I'll write to you,' said Edmund. 'And you know when I do, it'll be good news.'

There was only one thing he could mean. She never thought she'd ever dread receiving a letter from him. Fanny would have to work hard to get used to the idea of Edmund being engaged to Mary. With that, she went on her way with William, back to the house and family into which she was born.

CHAPTER TWENTY-THREE

Their journey had been long, but they'd talked non-stop the whole way. Just knowing Mansfield Park was behind Fanny made her feel better. William knew about Henry, and though he wished Fanny could love him (he was at an age where he felt strongly about love) he didn't talk about it because he knew it upset her.

As they approached the house Fanny was all hope and anxiety. A young boy of about eleven rushed out and met William, looking at Fanny once or twice and allowing her to kiss him as she got out of the carriage. Then she saw her mother and knew she loved that face. No less because it reminded her of her aunt Bertram. Fanny was taken into the narrow passage and drawing room, expecting another door because the room was so small, but then realised there wasn't one. Her mother hugged her tightly, with all the warmth and affection Fanny could hope for, until she rushed back out and started speaking to William.

'Don't you worry about me – Fanny's inside. Haven't you seen how well she's grown?' said William.

They both now entered the room and she hugged Fanny again, before commenting on her height and going back to William. Fanny's two sisters – Susan, fourteen, and Betsey, five – hung back at the door.

'You must both be so tired!' exclaimed the mother. 'Betsey, get Rebecca to put the kettle on and bring the tea! Just look at this sad fire – come closer,' she said to Fanny. 'Or you'll freeze. Susan, *you* should've taken care of the fire.'

'I was upstairs, moving my things,' said Susan in such a defensive tone that it startled Fanny.

There was a general bustle with the driver wanting to get paid, the youngest son, Sam, trying

to take Fanny's trunk upstairs by himself, and Mr Price walking in. Fanny got up, ready to meet her father, but he simply went up to William and shook his hand.

'Good to have you back, my boy! The doctor's been asking about you, he's got one of those boats. I wouldn't be surprised if you had your orders to sail tomorrow, but you can't sail in this wind . . .'

And on he went, until William said, 'But here's my sister, Fanny. It's so dark you don't see her.'

'Oh,' was simply his reply.

He went to meet her, commented that she'd grown into a woman with, 'You'll be wanting a husband soon, I suppose.' Before going back to talking to William about sailing.

Fanny felt depressed at her father's meeting and the strong smell of alcohol on him. There was still no sign of tea, and so William went to get changed, which was soon followed by two muddy-faced boys running into the room. Tom and Charles were kissed tenderly by their sister, but it was Tom Fanny wanted to keep close by, because she remembered looking after him when he was a baby. Tom, unfortunately, had other ideas. The boys sprinted out of the room, slamming the parlour door so many times Fanny got a headache.

'Rebecca! Mother!' called out William.

Something of his had gone missing, while Susan shouted, 'Mama! Tell Betsey the silver knife's *mine.*'

They had a sister who had died, and she had left a silver knife to Susan, but apparently Betsey was always taking it.

'Just let her have it. What do you want with it, anyway?' came Fanny's mother's voice.

Fanny was stunned. She was left alone in the room with her father, who'd picked up a newspaper and seemed to have forgotten she was there.

Her mother hadn't asked about Lady Bertram

or Mansfield Park. When guests came to Mansfield Park, questions were asked and enquiries made. It was just the proper thing to do. Fanny felt low, so she eventually went to her tiny bedroom. She couldn't help but compare it to the East Room in Mansfield Park, the room that everyone else felt too small for them. She went to sleep with a heavy heart and thought that perhaps tomorrow, the place would feel more like home.

Unfortunately, four days later, William was called to sail. He had to leave Fanny behind before they'd got to enjoy any of the quality time that they'd talked of.

'Look after Fanny, Mama,' he said to his mother. 'She's not like the rest of us.'

And he was gone. The home in which Fanny was now left was the exact opposite of everything she'd hoped for. Her father either ignored her or made her the punchline of a joke. He drank and smelled and hardly said a word that wasn't to do with the navy or ships.

But her mother was the biggest disappointment. Fanny wasn't shown any more affection than the first day she'd arrived. Her mother's heart was already full with her sons and Betsey, and spent most of her time bustling around the house without achieving anything.

Fanny tried to be useful around the house so she wouldn't be thought *better than the rest*. It was impossible to make an impression on the younger boys and as for Susan, Fanny never knew where her temper might fly. This was the home that was meant to have helped Fanny forget Mansfield Park and Edmund . . . Instead, she couldn't stop thinking about both. If Sir Thomas had known how desperate she felt, he'd have been sure that she would soon change her mind about Henry.

Now that she wasn't with Edmund, she knew Mary wouldn't write as often, but she never thought she'd look *forward* to Mary's letter. When one finally came, she read it with mixed feelings.

Dear Fanny,

Sorry it's been a while since I've written. Henry is away and that's probably why it's taken so long because I haven't had him on my back saying, 'Mary, when will you write to Fanny? Mary, aren't you going to write that letter?'

At last, I've seen Julia and Maria Rushworth, both of them looked very well, but especially Maria. I have to admit when I mentioned my brother's affection for you to Maria her face changed, which surprised me as I always thought she was better at keeping herself together. I suppose she will be on good form when she has a party at her house on Wimpole Street. A house that even Henry couldn't afford, so that might make her feel better.

Edmund isn't here yet, no doubt there's some old lady at his parsonage in Thornton Lacey keeping him.

∗ MANSFIELD PARK ∗

*Anyway, write back to me with a lovely letter which
will make Henry happy when he returns, and tell me
about all the captains you're ignoring for his sake.*

Yours,

Mary

The letter, odd as it was, connected her to people
she knew, and so it gave her comfort. There
certainly wasn't any comfort from the people in
Portsmouth.

Soon, though, Fanny realised that there was
one thing worth her making an effort: her sister,
Susan. Fanny found that her loud, temperamental
nature came from a place that wanted a sense of
justice in the household. There was a strength of
character in Susan that Fanny didn't have. If it
weren't for her, the family would probably be in
even worse condition. Susan looked up to Fanny,
and for the first time in her life Fanny realised she
was able to be of real help. She used some of the

money that Sir Thomas had given her to buy Betsey a new knife so that Susan could have the old one. Fanny, in her gentle way, would suggest things to Susan to try and bring out the best in her. The more Fanny saw the household, the more she was amazed that Susan managed to have such a mature understanding of things at all.

This was all a necessary distraction, now that Fanny had learnt from her aunt Bertram that Edmund had gone to London. Every day the postman brought along a fresh wave of terror. At least with Susan, she could forget about the inevitable, even if for only an hour or two.

CHAPTER TWENTY-FOUR

A few days had passed but Fanny hadn't heard anything. Perhaps Edmund and Mary were already engaged, and he was too happy to write.

It had been four weeks since Fanny had left Mansfield Park – she was keeping count of the days – when there was an unexpected knock on the door. Fanny froze when she heard the voice. There was no mistaking it: it was Henry Crawford.

In real times of distress, it seemed Fanny was able to keep herself together. She somehow managed to remember Henry's name well enough to introduce him to her mother as William's friend. But Fanny was terrified about what this meeting might lead to and she felt ready to die. While she was busy keeping herself alive, Henry was paying attention to her mother who, at least, was on her best form.

'Sorry Mr Price isn't here,' she said.

Fanny came back to earth long enough to feel very *un*-sorry about it. She hated herself for it, but she was ashamed of her home and even more ashamed of her father. Henry looked at Fanny. She was able to answer him well enough, considering, and listened to him as he passed on Mary's love and told her that Edmund had been in town for a few days. So, it must be settled, thought Fanny, who had prepared herself and so only felt a faint blush.

'It's a very fine morning,' said Henry. 'Perfect for a walk, if you wouldn't mind?'

Mrs Price told him that she never had time for a walk.

'Then your daughters?' he added, looking at Fanny.

'Oh no, it's not very nice out, they ought to stay home,' she answered.

But it was eventually settled and before Fanny knew it, she and Susan were out with Henry, walking to the high street. It was pain after pain, confusion after confusion, especially when she saw her father approaching them, looking like he'd had too much to drink. Fanny knew Henry's feelings would change after he'd met all her family, and though she'd been hoping for him to forget her, it was the worst way to have put him off. There are probably very few women who would not rather put up with being loved by a clever, charming man, than having him driven away by her dysfunctional family. Thankfully, and much to Fanny's surprise, her father was very polite. He even suggested he show Henry the dockyard, who was very keen about it, even though he'd seen it thirteen times already.

Henry had been looking for a chance to speak

to Fanny properly, but even when her father saw a friend and left them, her sister, Susan, was still with them. And, unlike Lady Bertram, she was sharp-eyed and eared.

'I was in Norfolk because I suspected my agent was being very unfair to my tenants,' said Henry. 'But I fixed it,' he added pointedly to Fanny.

'I'm so pleased you went to help people who really needed it,' she replied, truly moved by this.

He might not turn out so badly, Fanny thought, but that didn't change her feelings. Henry,

noticing Fanny's colour rise to her cheeks, started talking about Mansfield. *This* was a subject she longed to discuss with *anyone*. He talked of how much he'd loved it there, and how much he looked forward to returning. He mentioned Edmund, and Fanny kicked herself for not asking for more information and whether he had seen Mary or not.

As they walked home, Henry managed to whisper to Fanny that he had come to Portsmouth only to see her. She was sorry for the trouble he'd taken, and believed that she saw there was a real change in his manner – he seemed genuinely altered since she last saw him. Towards the end of their walk, Henry linked arms with her and her sister on each side and she was grateful for him for she was tired after so much time outside. She was feeling the effects of not having regular exercise. He looked at her when he could, and though still beautiful, he worried that Fanny wasn't at her healthiest.

'You're here for two months?' he asked.

'Yes, and it's almost been a full month,' replied Fanny.

'I see. I'd have thought six weeks would've been enough here.' He turned to Susan to explain. 'I mean, I don't think your sister is getting the exercise and air she needs for her health.' He turned back to Fanny. 'If you need to go back to Mansfield Park, then all you have to do is hint to Mary and me, and we will come and take you.'

Fanny tried to laugh it off and said there was no need.

'I'm serious,' he added.

'Honestly, I'm quite well,' she replied, distressed at his attention.

They reached home but he wouldn't leave her. 'I wish you were in better health. Can I get you anything from town?'

'No, thank you.'

'Is there any message you want to give to anyone?' he asked.

'My love to your sister,' she said. 'And if you see Edmund, tell him I'm looking forward to hearing from him.'

'I will. And if he doesn't write to you, I'll write his excuses for him.'

And so he left. Fanny felt a new low. She was half-glad not to have to see Henry again, and half in pain, as if she were separated from Mansfield all over again. Then to know he'd be in London with

Edmund and Mary almost made her envious to a point where she hated herself.

She was only glad to see such an improvement in Henry himself. He was calmer and more thoughtful and as such, surely, he'd stop pursuing her.

CHAPTER TWENTY-FIVE

Dear Fanny,

I write to tell you that after Henry saw you in Portsmouth and met your family, he was just as taken by your pretty looks as ever. I'm not sure what else to write – I wish you were here! I'd talk to you until you were exhausted. But it's impossible to put what I am thinking and feeling on to paper, so I'll leave you to guess what you like.

I should've sent you a letter after the party at Maria's I had told you about, but it was so long ago now that it's hardly worth noting. All I'll say is that she looked very fine, and it was a very fine do. The friend I am staying with, Lady Fraser, adored

∗ JANE AUSTEN ∗

Maria's house and it wouldn't exactly make me *miserable either. Lady Fraser's husband isn't as bad-looking as I had imagined, but he is nothing compared to Edmund Bertram. There, I mentioned him — but it'd be suspicious if I didn't. We've met two or three times and had a dinner together. He was the most distinguished looking of everyone, and there were sixteen of us. Anyway, must go now, dear Fanny,*

Yours affectionately —

I almost forgot (Edmund's fault, he gets into my head more than is good) — I will be ready at once if you want to go back to Mansfield Park early. Lastly, Henry's going to Norfolk on some business that you apparently approve of, but I'm making him stay until after a party of mine — a man like Henry can't be spared at such events. He'll see the Rushworths, which I'm looking forward to, and I think he might be a little curious himself, though he won't admit it.

What a strange letter! It didn't matter how many times Fanny read it, nothing was clear. Except that Edmund had not proposed. Why did Mary only talk about his looks but nothing of *who he was*? And her scheme to get Henry to see Maria was the worst judged scheme of them all.

Fanny became impatient for another letter. She couldn't concentrate on anything. And why was it that Edmund *still* hadn't written? To distract herself, she gave all her attention to Susan. The idea that one day, she would have to leave her sister behind in this household distressed Fanny. If only she could've returned Henry Crawford's love – she felt sure that he'd think it was an excellent idea to get Susan out of Portsmouth, too.

Three weeks later, a letter from Edmund finally arrived. It was so long that Fanny readied herself to read all about how happy he was that Mary and he were engaged.

My dear Fanny,

Sorry for not writing sooner. Henry gave me your message, but I couldn't write in London and hoped you'd understand my silence. If there were happy news I'd have sent you a few lines, but I'm back at Mansfield Park with no news to share. I know Mary writes to you, but I don't think there's any conflict in sharing my feelings. There's comfort in knowing we both share a friend.

I was in London for three weeks and saw Miss Crawford often. The Frasers were good to me, but I did not like Lady Fraser at all, and, I'm afraid, Miss Crawford was changed. Lady Fraser seemed cold-hearted and vain, and I don't think it's been good for Mary to be around such shallow people.

And yet, I can't give Miss Crawford up, Fanny. I can't imagine having any other woman as a wife – and I wouldn't say this if I didn't think she cared for me too. If I lose her, my only comfort is that it will be because I'm not rich enough, not because I'm a clergyman.

I've met with Crawford several times and he still loves you. When he met with Maria, I couldn't help but think of what you'd told me. She was cold and he seemed surprised. I feel Maria is happy and Julia is enjoying London in a way I couldn't. But my enjoyment at Mansfield Park is even less. We miss you terribly and talk about you every hour.

Are you happy in Portsmouth? You've been away too long! My father will come and collect you but probably not until after Easter. I can't have you go away like this every year, Fanny. I can't make any changes at Thornton Lacey without knowing if I'll have a wife there living with me. I will write to Mary. I think I must tell her my true feelings.

I am yours, as ever, my dearest Fanny.

'I'll never wish for a letter again,' said Fanny to herself.

Everything in the letter agitated, even angered Fanny. How could she wait until after Easter? And

Edmund was blind to all Mary's faults and blamed the people around her. *He thinks she actually cares for someone other than herself and her brother! Write to her, Edmund! Get it over with. Marry her and condemn yourself to misery.*

Fanny had to check her thoughts. They were too resentful, and after a while, her heart softened. Edmund was simply too kind to everyone. It was only a few days later that Fanny received a letter from her aunt Bertram telling her some distressing news. Tom had been taken ill after having had too much to drink and taking a fall in London. Edmund had gone to bring him back to Mansfield Park.

He is not the same Tom, dear Fanny! wrote her aunt. *He looks pale and sick and Sir Thomas says the journey has made him worse . . . Oh, how we miss you!*

Fanny was sorry for everyone! Sorry she couldn't be there to help her aunt, who for once sounded truly troubled. Susan was the only one who cared and listened to Fanny, who was now receiving a letter about Tom every day. It was difficult for Mrs Price to care about a family that lived over a hundred miles away. And poor Fanny could do nothing but wait for more news.

CHAPTER TWENTY-SIX

After a week, Tom's fever had improved and Lady Bertram was soon sure that everything would be well. Edmund's letters to Fanny, though, suggested Tom was not yet out of danger. They worried about his lungs.

Edmund was looking after his brother – Tom wanted no one else – and this made Edmund seem even kinder than Fanny had ever imagined. Unfortunately, even while caring for his brother Edmund still wrote about Mary. He'd decided against writing a letter and was going to go to London to speak to her when Tom was better. But his brother's recovery was very slow.

Easter came and went, and Fanny had now been in Portsmouth for three months. Her aunt wished for her, but Fanny never got word from Sir Thomas about when he might come and collect her. She now realised that Mansfield Park was truly her home. And when she'd read from her aunt Bertram's letters, 'I hope you shall never be away from home again,' Fanny finally felt a sense of belonging. She wondered why Maria and Julia hadn't gone home after hearing of Tom's illness. Apparently, Julia had written to ask whether she should, but it seemed clear she'd prefer to remain where she was.

It had been weeks since Fanny had heard from Mary, until a letter finally came:

My dear Fanny,

Forgive me for my long silence, even though I don't deserve it, but I write to you to ask how things are at Mansfield Park. I am very sorry for Tom Bertram — at first, I thought he was just making a fuss, but it

*seems that he is genuinely in bad health. Is this true?
Poor Sir Thomas will feel the loss heavily! Fanny . . .
stop with that cunning look, but I will only say that
should the worst happen, then there will be one less
poor man in the world! And no one could deserve that
wealth more than Edmund. He might not have
'Esquire' after his name, but my affections are so
strong I could overlook more than that.*

Yours ever —

*I'd begun folding my letter when Henry walked in.
He saw Maria Rushworth this morning, who confirms
that Mr Bertram is in decline. Now, don't be jealous,
Henry only has eyes for you. Even now, he's repeating
what he offered about taking you from Portsmouth to
Mansfield Park. I can't repeat everything Henry is
saying to me right now — just know that he is full of
affection for you.*

Fanny was disgusted with most of the letter, but
felt the pull of potentially being back at Mansfield

Park in three days. But she couldn't owe a favour to a woman like Mary! And Henry, who she had thought had changed, was still seeing Maria and probably flirting as much as ever. She'd never met such selfish people before. She knew she had to decline Henry's offer. As for Tom's health, she reported what she knew, which was exactly what Mary had probably been hoping to hear. If Tom died, then Mary would forgive Edmund for being a clergyman because he'd inherit a fortune. It was clear: nothing mattered more to Mary than money.

Fanny believed she might receive another letter from Mary, telling her that she'd been granted permission by Sir Thomas to come and collect Fanny and bring her home, but the next letter she received from her was very different.

Something very disturbing has reached me, dear Fanny, and I'm writing to you to ignore all *of it in case it spreads. Henry is blameless — aside from a little temptation — and thinks of no one but you! I'm sure it'll all be fine, and it is just Mr Rushworth being silly. I bet they're gone to Mansfield Park with Julia. But why wouldn't you have us come for you? Yours —*

Fanny was horrified. Since no news had reached her, she could only assume what the letter meant — that Mr Crawford and Maria's behaviour had caused a scandal. She couldn't care less about Henry, but what would happen if the news reached Mansfield Park? She could only hope that the Rushworths *had* gone to Mansfield. For a little while, Fanny had truly thought that Henry had felt for her in a way that was out of the ordinary. She hoped he'd now realise he was incapable of being steady in his love for any woman.

The following day no new letter came. All was just as usual; when her father walked in with his newspaper, her mother was complaining about the carpet and the boys were banging about in the passage. Fanny was startled when her father said, 'What's the name of your cousins in London?'

'Maria and Julia.'

'Well! They've got a lot to answer for,' he exclaimed and shoved the paper in front of Fanny.

'Your relations aren't so fine now, are they? Dunno what your Sir Thomas is like, but if she were my daughter, I'd give her and that man a good beating.'

Fanny read the article:

It is with concern that we announce a marital scandal in the Rushworth family of Wimpole Street. Mrs Rushworth, who had promised to be a leading lady in the fashionable world, seems to have left her husband with the well-known and charming Mr Crawford. It is not known where they are gone . . .

'It's a mistake,' said Fanny. 'They must mean someone else.'

Fanny felt despair but spoke firmly to hide the whole thing from her family as long as possible. She knew the truth as soon as she'd read it, though. Her father shrugged.

'I hope it's not true,' said Mrs Price, but was

soon distracted. 'How many times do I have to tell Rebecca about fixing the carpet!'

Fanny suddenly realised: Mary hadn't been talking about Mr and Mrs Rushworth going to Mansfield Park, but about Maria Rushworth and Henry! She couldn't sleep all night. She thought about everyone who'd be affected by Henry's selfish vanity and Maria's unprincipled attachment. How would Edmund take it? What would it mean for Mary . . .?

Days passed without any more information, until a letter finally came with a stamp from London and Edmund's name.

Dear Fanny,

You know everything and I hope God is giving you the support I cannot. We've been in London for two days but can't find them. And you might have heard of the last blow. Julia has eloped with Tom's friend, John Yates. My father is distressed but not so

*much that he can't act. He's asked to bring you home
for my mother's sake. I'll be there tomorrow morning.
He also asks that you bring Susan – you can settle it
with your family as you see fit.*

Yours –

Edmund arrived at eight o'clock in the morning.
She went to meet him and he held on to her so
that she could hear the beating of his heart. 'My
Fanny! My only comfort.'

They remained like this for a few moments
before he stood back and collected himself, trying
to keep his voice firm. Everything was readied as
the rest of the family sat down for breakfast and
they said goodbye to Fanny in the same detached
way they had welcomed her. This time, Fanny left
with her sister, Susan. Their parents were happy to
let her go.

Fanny's heart swelled with joy as they left
Portsmouth, but the journey was a silent one, as

Edmund couldn't say much in front of Susan. The following day they were alone before they set off again and Edmund noticed how pale Fanny had become. He thought it was because of Henry, not because she'd been living under her parents' roof for so long. He took her hand.

'You must feel so betrayed, and by someone who claimed to love you so much,' he said. 'But what you felt was so new compared to . . . think how I must feel, Fanny. We must bear our pain bravely.'

They finally arrived at Mansfield Park. Fanny couldn't help but admire its beauty; she had last seen it when it was winter, and now it was spring,

it was even more beautiful. She watched Edmund with his eyes closed, as if shutting out his home and the world. They entered the house and Fanny heard footsteps – ones that had never been taken so quickly. Her aunt Bertram came towards her and hugged her tightly. 'Dear Fanny! You're here at last. Now I shall be well again.'

CHAPTER TWENTY-SEVEN

Everyone was miserable, but no one more so than Mrs Norris. Maria was her favourite and the match had been her doing – as she liked to regularly tell people – so its outcome truly afflicted her. She felt nothing but irritation towards Fanny. She was sure that if Fanny had married Henry, *this* would not have happened. As for Susan, Mrs Norris regarded her as an intruder, like a spy. But Susan was taught never to expect anything but harshness from Mrs Norris, so this was bearable, especially since her aunt Bertram was ready to be kind to her because she was Fanny's sister.

Now that Fanny had returned to her, Lady

Bertram felt able to relive all the ways the whole affair was terrible. Fanny could only imagine what her uncle must be feeling. She learnt that Maria had been in Twickenham with some friends while Mr Rushworth went to Bath to bring his mother to London. Her friends' homes were open to Henry at all times and Mr Rushworth's jealousy returned to him ten-fold.

It seemed to Fanny that every child of Sir Thomas's was a disappointment to him but Edmund: Maria's scandal, Tom's illness that was a result of his own poor lifestyle, Julia's elopement and its timing! But she didn't know that Edmund still brought Sir Thomas some anxiety. At any other time, his marriage to Mary Crawford would've been a great connection, but now it felt impossible. Had he known the things Mary had said to Edmund when they met in London, he wouldn't have wanted her for a daughter-in-law, even if she had forty thousand pounds.

It was after the fourth day of being home that Edmund finally opened up to Fanny. It was raining, and Lady Bertram had just cried herself to sleep, so the two of them were more or less alone.

'Fanny, she asked to meet with me. Her friend begged me to come, and so I went to what felt like our last meeting. How can I repeat how she spoke? She said, "I don't want to defend Henry at your sister's expense," which was bad enough, but she went on as if it was just a minor mistake. And only then because it had been found out ... . She didn't see how improper it was!'

He paused, as if lost in his own thoughts.

'And what did you say?' asked Fanny.

He shook his head. 'Nothing. I was stunned. She started to talk about you — at least she did you justice, but then she always had — that he would never find a woman like you again. I hope this isn't painful to hear? I'll stop if it is.'

Fanny told him to go on.

'But then she said, "If only Fanny had said yes to him. They'd have been busy making wedding arrangements and he'd have been too happy to give any attention to Maria. It would've all just ended in yearly flirtations between the two and nothing more!" Can you believe it, Fanny? I finally see her for who she is.'

'I'm sorry,' said Fanny.

Edmund shook his head. 'I'd have preferred double the heartbreak to thinking of her like I do now. I told her, too.' He paused. 'I told her that I had been mistaken – that I had been thinking of her not as she is, but as I imagined her to be. She became very red and eventually managed to say something laughingly about being lectured. She tried, but she couldn't hide how she felt.

So, I wished sincerely that she might rethink her own principles and that she might find happiness.'

Over the coming days, their conversations kept coming back to Mary, how she'd captured his heart, how hurt he was, until Fanny felt it right to tell him what Mary had written about Tom in the letter. Poor Edmund! He felt certain he would never love like this again. He only had Fanny in his heart as his dear friend, nothing more.

CHAPTER TWENTY-EIGHT

Let other pens dwell on guilt and misery. Some time had passed, and things began to settle. Fanny was of use in the place she loved, and Edmund was no longer going to marry a woman who would have been bad for him.

Sir Thomas came back home and looked at his niece in a new light.

'Fanny, you have shown great maturity and respect in all things,' he said and hugged her. She would no longer be scared by him, but would love him, just as he seemed to love her. Edmund was far from happy, but she knew that in the end, the right thing had happened. Sir Thomas suffered the most and the longest. Mrs Norris had spoiled the girls, so he had been strict with them to balance it out. So strict that they never showed their true colours to him and he never had the chance to correct their thinking. All the expensive education in the world didn't teach them how to be humble and understand what was morally right.

Soon, Sir Thomas came to see things weren't all bad. Julia was embarrassed by what she (and her sister) had done and Mr Yates was so keen to please Sir Thomas that he might not be the worst son-in-law, after all. Julia had been used to being second best to Maria, so thought less of herself and was able to be guided a bit more easily. Tom also recovered his health and was so horrified by what had happened with Maria that he finally began to think about someone other than himself. Soon enough, even Edmund's pain began to lessen. Many summer evenings were spent where he spoke to Fanny about his feelings and slowly, he began to be his old self again.

Maria refused to leave Henry and was convinced they'd get married. It was a long time before she realised that would never happen. Mr Rushworth managed to get a divorce easily enough and would probably end up getting married again. What would happen to Maria was another question. Sir Thomas would not have her back home and Mrs Norris accused Fanny of being the reason for his indifference. Sir Thomas assured Mrs Norris that he'd look after Maria, but she had decided her own fate and he wasn't going to allow her back into their neighbourhood.

Mrs Norris was so attached to her dear niece that she left Mansfield Park. She and Maria were set up together in a place where there was no love on one side and no judgement on the other. Sir Thomas could not have been more glad to have Mrs Norris leave. He didn't know how he had put up with her for so long.

Even Fanny couldn't manage to be sorry about it. If Henry had carried on pursuing Fanny as he had done, uprightly, saying and doing all the right things he would probably have won her over. Edmund would've married Mary, and Fanny and Henry's marriage would probably have followed. But instead of going back to Norfolk as he had promised Fanny, he stayed in London because he wanted to see Mrs Rushworth, and when he did, he couldn't bear her coldness. So, he began his pursuit, broke her down with his flirtations, not understanding how much she loved him. He was desperate to keep it all a secret – Maria had other plans though. He got caught up and took off with her, but still thought of Fanny, even in that moment. He knew he would never meet a woman like her again.

It was a happy coincidence that Dr Grant was offered a new parsonage in London, so the Grants could leave Mansfield Park. This way, Mary was able to go and live with her sister once more, and she stayed on even after Dr Grant had died (after a few too many heavy dinners one week). She was determined to never fall in love with a younger brother again. Still, it didn't matter how many men were intrigued by her beauty and her twenty-thousand-pound dowry, there was no man who could put the handsome Edmund Bertram out of her head.

In this sense, Edmund was better off. He didn't have to wait long to find someone who was worthy – *worthier* – of his love. After all the time he'd spent telling Fanny that he'd never find another woman like Mary, he began to realise that there *was* a woman who would, in fact, be better in every way. Fanny had become dearer to him than ever and he began to be hopeful that her affection for him might turn into something more. Edmund stopped thinking of Mary Crawford and started being as anxious about making Fanny his wife as she could want him to be. Even when Edmund had loved Mary, he saw that Fanny's mind was superior. In fact, he felt Fanny was too good for him, but since one doesn't mind having what is too good for one, he was very steady in his pursuit. Imagine his feelings when he found out that all this time Fanny had loved *him*.

Sir Thomas had become sick of worldly connections and appreciated more and more the importance of real character and principles when it came to happiness. He forgot how he'd once felt about Fanny's low status and gave both her and Edmund his blessing. This is how time and experience can change people's minds.

Lady Bertram couldn't bear the thought of parting with Fanny, but this was soon overcome by the fact that Susan had taken Fanny's place. Susan, who was eager to please and had a quick mind and a fearless personality, fitted in as easily as could be expected. Lady Bertram soon enough became so fond of Susan that she even *preferred* her to Fanny.

Now that the parsonage was again available, there was no reason why Edmund and Fanny should not move there. It used to be a place that

Fanny entered with pain, thinking of what had passed, but it now became as dear to her as Mansfield Park.

A NOTE FROM AYISHA

I read my first Austen book, *Emma*, when I was fifteen. I'd taken it to a cousin's wedding, which lasted – as with most Asian weddings – about eight days. The ardent obsession with marriage – and marrying well – has not yet dwindled in South Asian homes. (Just recently, at a wedding, an aunt asked what I say to men to put them off, given I'm not married yet. I told her that usually being myself is enough.) Austen would have come up with something better – partly because she wouldn't have been distracted by the ladoos (special Asian sweetmeats) like I was.

I took an Austen module when I was reading English Literature at university and we were asked to write a short story, capturing her humour, addressing Austenian themes, whilst setting it in modern Britain. It only struck me then, quite forcibly, that being Pakistani was often like being in an Austen novel; chaperones are sometimes involved when dating, there are strict rules about what you are and aren't allowed to do before getting married, not to mention intrusive families and an obsession with how much money the man you're marrying has.

At each stage of life, I have read, and reread, Austen's books – including those she wrote in her youth – finding myself (and others) in her descriptions and characters, and being able to laugh at the absurdity of what we Asian women suffer under the tyranny of nosy aunts.

Austen has been my travelling wedding companion (*Pride and Prejudice* and *Mansfield Park* both accompanied me to weddings in Pakistan). To me, she is current and timeless; a balm for my soul; an inspiration in dealing with difficult themes with a light touch. She is the reason I often ask, *What would Austen do?*

And every time I know – she'd create comedy out of it.

A NOTE FROM ÉGLANTINE

My name is Églantine Ceulemans, and as you
might have noticed thanks to my first name . . .
I am French!

In France, we tend to associate Britain with
wonderful English gardens, a unique sense of
humour, William Shakespeare and, last but not
least, Jane Austen!

It was such an honour to have the opportunity

to illustrate Jane Austen's stories. I have always enjoyed reading books that are filled with love, laughter and happy endings, and Austen writes all of those things brilliantly. And who wouldn't love to illustrate gorgeous dresses, stunning mansions and passionate young women standing up for their deep convictions? I also tried to do justice to Austen's humour and light-heartedness by drawing characterful people and adding in friendly pets (sometimes well-hidden and always witnessing intense but mostly funny situations!).

I discovered Jane Austen's work with *Pride and Prejudice* one sun-filled summer, and I have such good memories of sitting reading it in the garden beneath my grandmother's weeping willow. This setting definitely helped me to fall in love with the book, but it would be a lie to say that I wasn't moved by Elizabeth and Mr Darcy's love story and that I didn't laugh when her mother tried (with no shame at all) to marry her daughters to all the best catches in the town! I imagined all those characters in my head so vividly, and it was a real pleasure to finally illustrate them, alongside all Austen's other amazing characters.

Jane Austen is an author who managed to depict nineteenth-century England with surprising modernity. She questioned the morality of so-called well-to-do people and she managed to write smartly, sharply and independently, at a time where women were considered to be nothing if not married to a man. I hope that these illustrated versions of her books will help you to question the past and the present, without ever forgetting to laugh … and to dream!

SO, WHO WAS JANE AUSTEN?

Jane Austen was born in 1775 and had seven siblings. Her parents were well-respected in their local community, and her father was the clergyman for a nearby parish. She spent much of her life helping to run the family home, whilst reading and writing in her spare time.

* JANE AUSTEN *

Jane began to anonymously publish her work in her thirties and four of her novels were released during her lifetime: *Sense and Sensibility*, *Pride and Prejudice*, *Mansfield Park* and *Emma*. However, at the age of forty-one she became ill, eventually dying in 1817. Her two remaining novels, *Northanger Abbey* and *Persuasion*, were published after her death.

Austen's books are well-known for their comedy, wit and irony. Her observations about wealthy society, and especially the role women played in it, were unlike anything that had been published before. Her novels were not widely read or praised until years later, but they have gone on to leave a mark on the world for ever, inspiring countless poems, books, plays and films.

AND WHAT WAS IT LIKE IN 1814?

WERE BIG FAMILIES COMMON?

It was very common for families during the Regency era to have multiple children. Jane Austen herself had seven siblings and Fanny Dashwood is one of nine children. At this time, the rate of infant mortality was higher than it is today, so parents often wanted more children to ensure they would be looked after in old age! Having a large family could also mean that there were extra hands to help around the house and on the farm, allowing poorer families to be able to earn more.

WAS IT NORMAL FOR COUSINS TO MARRY EACH OTHER DURING THIS PERIOD?

A long time before Jane Austen was alive, in 1540, King Henry VIII passed the Marriage Act, which made marriage legal between first cousins. By the 1880s, marriage between cousins was not seen as unusual, although it was more common in wealthier families due to a desire to keep property within the family at the point of inheritance. At the time of Jane Austen writing *Mansfield Park*, there would have been nothing shocking about Fanny and Edmund's relationship even though today it is very unusual for cousins to marry.

HOW POPULAR WAS THE THEATRE?

The theatre during the Regency era was a popular pastime and was visited regularly by those who spent seasons in London. People would dress up for the occasion in hopes of showing off and impressing other theatregoers. Renting or owning a box (the best seats in the theatre) was a sign of your social status but only the wealthy could afford to do so.

However, actors were viewed as being very low on the social ladder — the theatre was not considered to be a respectable career path. Actresses were completely frowned upon and many people believed that women should not be allowed to act at all. Edmund is of this opinion at the start of the novel and attempts to stop his family and friends from putting on the play, *Lover's Vows*.

WHY WAS LOVER'S VOWS SEEN AS INAPPROPRIATE AT THE TIME?

The play, *Lover's Vows*, that the characters in *Mansfield Park* are rehearsing was a real play, but we don't know whether Jane Austen ever saw it performed. At the time, society viewed it to be a shocking play, so it is no surprise that Sir Thomas bans his family from performing it. Putting on such a play could have caused problems for his otherwise respectable household's reputation.

COLLECT THEM ALL!

AWESOMELY AUSTEN

JANE AUSTEN'S

PERSUASION

WITTY WORDS BY NARINDER DHAMI
DELIGHTFUL DOODLES BY ÉGLANTINE CEULEMANS

AWESOMELY AUSTEN

JANE AUSTEN'S

SENSE AND
SENSIBILITY

WITTY WORDS BY JOANNA NADIN
DELIGHTFUL DOODLES BY ÉGLANTINE CEULEMANS

AWESOMELY AUSTEN

JANE AUSTEN'S

NORTHANGER
ABBEY

WITTY WORDS BY STEVEN BUTLER
DELIGHTFUL DOODLES BY ÉGLANTINE CEULEMANS